D0121273

C0000 002 743 345

# Also By Jim Eldridge

*WRESTLING TROLLS* series:
*Match 1: Big Rock and the Masked
  Avenger*
*Match 2: Hunk and Thud*
*Match 3: The Giant Rumble*
*Match 4: Thud in Trouble*

*Disgusting Dave* series
And many more . . .

# JIM ELDRIDGE

**WRESTLING TROLLS**

MATCH
5

# JACK VERSUS VETO

Illustrated by JAN BIELECKI

HOT
KEY
BOOKS

First published in Great Britain in 2015 by Hot Key Books
Northburgh House, 10 Northburgh Street, London EC1V 0AT

Text copyright © Jim Eldridge 2015
Illustration copyright © Jan Bielecki 2015

The moral rights of the author and illustrator have been asserted.

All rights reserved.
No part of this publication may be reproduced, stored or transmitted
in any form by any means, electronic, mechanical, photocopying or
otherwise, without the prior written permission of the publisher.

All characters in this publication are fictitious and any resemblance to real
persons, living or dead, is purely coincidental.

A CIP catalogue record for this book is available from the British Library.

ISBN: 978-1-4714-0267-8

1

This book is typeset in 14pt Sabon using Atomik ePublisher

Printed and bound by Clays Ltd, St Ives Plc

www.hotkeybooks.com

Hot Key Books is part of the Bonnier Publishing Group
www.bonnierpublishing.com

# Contents

# RUSTLERS

# CHAPTER 1

The crowd inside Bun Village Hall was small, but very enthusiastic. Jack and Milo sat with Blaze in the front row and listened to the crowd cheer loudly as Big Rock and his opponent, a troll called Block, clambered into the ring.

'What I like about this place is that it's nice and friendly,' said Milo. 'There's no sneaky cheating, like when Lord Veto's orcs are taking part. Look at how good-natured the Fighting Pink Fairy was, even though the Masked Avenger beat her.'

They were here for the Great Bun Wrestle Smackdown. Despite its grand-sounding name, the Great Bun Wrestle Smackdown was a very small event with just two bouts taking place:

Big Rock against Block, and the Masked Avenger against the Fighting Pink Fairy, a girl wrestler who dressed up in a pink fairy costume, complete with pink pretend wings.

The Masked Avenger had defeated the Fighting Pink Fairy by two pinfalls to one. As Milo said, it had been a good-natured contest, and the Fairy had even given the Masked Avenger a present of her pink wings, in appreciation of her wrestling skills.

Usually, the Masked Avenger – who was actually Princess Ava, the teenage ruler of the Kingdom of Weevil – and her dresser, Meenu, came in their own caravan, but this time they had travelled to Bun with Milo and the gang. This had resulted in grumbles from Robin, the old horse, about the extra weight he was hauling.

'Big Rock offered to pull the caravan for you part of the way to give you a rest,' Jack had pointed out.

'That wouldn't be right,' Robin had said sniffily. 'My job as a horse is to pull the caravan. Big Rock's job is to wrestle.'

'Yes, but we share the work,' Jack had insisted. 'We help one another. That's what a family does.'

When they'd arrived they'd left Robin to rest and graze on the village green, while they headed for the hall where the Smackdown was to be held.

'This is what wrestling should be like,' said Milo. 'Done in a proper, sporting way, with everyone sticking to the rules, and no nastiness.'

The referee climbed into the ring between the ropes and walked to the centre.

'Ladies and gentlemen!' he announced. 'It gives me enormous pleasure to introduce the two contestants for the second bout of this fantastic Great Bun Wrestle Smackdown! In the blue corner, the Troll Champion, Big Rock!'

The crowd cheered loudly, and some of them chanted, 'Big Rock! Big Rock! Big Rock!'

'Big Rock isn't the Troll Champion,' Jack whispered to Milo. 'That's Crush!'

'Okay, I may have exaggerated a little when I made the booking,' whispered back Milo.

'You lied,' said Jack accusingly. 'All that talk about "no cheating" . . .'

'I didn't actually *lie*!' whispered back Milo. 'After all, here in Bun, Big Rock *is* the Troll Champion.'

'Only because there are only two Wrestling Trolls here, and Big Rock's won more bouts than Block,' pointed out Jack.

'Exactly,' nodded Milo.

'Huh!' snorted Jack disapprovingly.

Above them, in the ring, the referee was introducing the other wrestler.

'And in the red corner, please give a huge Bun welcome to his opponent, that fantastic Wrestling Troll, Block!'

Again, the crowd cheered and shouted their support, chanting Block's name.

Block was a tall, heavily muscled Wrestling Troll, with spiky grass sticking out of his skull as if it was hair. He was younger than Big Rock, and his rocky body shone as light reflected off the quartz and granite that showed beneath his sparkling blue-and-black costume. Big Rock's costume was old and faded with so much mending that it looked like a patchwork quilt. On the front was an embroidered picture of a mountaintop, which Jack had only just recently sewn back on.

'Block's a new wrestler on the circuit,' murmured Milo. 'He's keen to make his mark and get noticed. It should be a good contest.'

'Gentlemen, return to your corners!' said the referee.

He waited until the two Trolls were in their corners, then gave a thumbs up to his assistant, and the bell for round one went *Ding!*

The two Wrestling Trolls came out from their corners and began to circle one another warily.

'Come on, Big Rock!' called Jack.

It was Block who made the first move, suddenly launching himself at Big Rock with a dive. Big Rock swivelled to one side and let Block hurtle past him. He caught Block round the waist and was about to crash him to the canvas when Block did a forward roll, dragging Big Rock with him.

There was a blur of rock and quartz and coloured costumes, and then Big Rock was flat on his back in the middle of the ring with Block lying across his head, pinning his shoulders down.

'One!' counted the referee. 'Two! Three!'

Block rolled off Big Rock and waved at the crowd, acknowledging their cheers and applause.

'Block's good,' murmured Jack admiringly. 'That was a really fast move.'

The contest restarted, and once again Block tried the same move, attempting to drag Big Rock with him as he did a forward roll, but this time Big Rock was ready. Big Rock plonked himself down in the middle of the ring and let Block roll and, as the young troll bounced to his feet, Big Rock jumped forward, catching Block off balance.

*Thump!*

Block hit the canvas face first. Big Rock grabbed Block by the legs and tried to turn him over onto his back, but Block managed to twist and slip his way out of Big Rock's grasp and retreated to his own corner.

'This is harder than Big Rock thought it would be,' muttered Jack.

'Big Rock will win,' said Milo confidently.

At that moment, Block threw himself at Big Rock, who stumbled backwards and tumbled through the ropes and out of the ring.

'I'm not so sure,' said Jack doubtfully as Big Rock climbed back in.

From then, the bout swung this way and that, first Block getting the upper hand, and then Big Rock.

The two pinfalls that ended the bout came in swift succession. The first came with Big Rock picking Block up and flipping him down and falling on him. The second came as Block jumped from the top rope to power a launching dive at Big Rock. But Big Rock ducked, letting Block fly over him, and then he threw himself after Block, grabbing him and throwing him onto his back on the canvas before Block could recover.

The two trolls shook hands as the referee announced Big Rock as the winner.

'Good wrestling,' Big Rock praised his opponent. 'Next time, bet you win.'

Block gave a big grin, and gave Big Rock a hug. Then both wrestlers walked around the ring, waving at the crowd and acknowledging their cheers, before climbing out.

'That was close,' said Jack.

'Block good,' nodded Big Rock.

'But you're better,' said the Masked Avenger, who'd just joined them.

'Big Rock's experience did the trick,' said Meenu. 'We watched you from the dressing room.'

The crowd were still cheering, and autograph books were being thrust at Big Rock.

Milo smiled.

'Time to sell some souvenirs,' he said.

\* \* \*

Together, and arm-in-arm, the gang walked jauntily away from the village hall and back towards the green, with Blaze flying overhead. As they walked, they sang:

'Wrestling Trolls,
Tum-di-dum!
Wrestling Trolls,
Tum-di-dum!'

'Wait till Robin hears what he missed!' chuckled Jack. 'Two great bouts, and two great victories!'

'He will be gutted!' agreed Milo.

They carried on singing and whistling happily as they approached the caravan.

'Robin!' called Jack.

There was no reply.

Blaze flew down and settled beside them.

'Robin's not here,' he said. 'I've just flown over the caravan and around the green.'

'That's strange,' frowned Milo. 'I wonder where he's gone.'

He spotted a small boy walking across the green.

'Excuse me, little boy!' he called. 'Have you seen a horse around?'

'An old horse,' put in Jack.

'A very old horse,' added the Masked Avenger.

'A horse?' asked the boy.

'Yes,' said Milo. 'He was here, with our caravan.'

The boy looked worried. 'You don't mean you left him alone!' he said, horrified.

'Yes,' said Jack. 'Why not?'

'He's old enough to look after himself,' said Meenu.

'Because of the rustlers,' said the boy.

'What rustlers?' asked Milo.

'They come into the village and steal horses,' said the boy. 'They're bad people.'

The gang looked at one another in horror.

'Horse thieves!' exclaimed Milo.

'Where do they come from?' asked the Masked Avenger.

The boy shook his head. 'My parents don't want me to talk about it, in case anything bad happens to us,' he said. 'No one here wants to talk about it.'

'But someone must know where they are!' exploded Milo.

'The Village Marshal,' said the boy. 'He knows.' He gave them an apologetic smile. 'I can't say any more. I'm not allowed to. And I have to get home.'

With that the boy ran off across the green.

'This bad!' growled Big Rock.

'Yes, and we're going to do something about it,' said Milo determinedly. 'Let's go and see this Village Marshal.'

'While you do that, Meenu, Blaze and I will go and look for Robin, and see if we can find out about who took him,' said the Masked Avenger.

'But what if you run into these horse thieves?' asked Jack, worried.

'If I do, they're going to regret stealing Robin!' scowled the Masked Avenger.

# CHAPTER 2

Milo, Jack and Big Rock found the Village Marshal in a small wooden shack on the other side of the green, not far from the village hall. A painted sign above the door said: TOM TUM. VILLAGE MARSHAL.

Milo pushed open the door and went in, followed by Jack and Big Rock. A short, thin man with a bald head and a big ginger moustache was sitting at a desk, his head bowed over a newspaper.

'Marshal Tum?' asked Milo.

'That's me,' nodded the man. Then he looked up, and as he saw Big Rock his face lit up into a smile.

'Hey!' he said. 'You're Big Rock, the

Wrestling Troll! I've just seen you wrestle! Great stuff!'

'Bad men take our horse,' said Big Rock bluntly.

The Marshal looked at Big Rock in surprise, and then his smile vanished and his face clouded over.

'Stolen?' he asked.

'Yes,' said Milo. 'Someone told us that horse thieves are operating here. That they come into the village and steal them.'

The Marshal shifted awkwardly in his chair. He looked very uncomfortable.

'Yes,' he said unhappily. 'They turn them into burgers and sell them to make money.'

'Burgers!' echoed Jack, shocked.

'People cat Robin?' said Big Rock, horrified.

'I'm afraid so,' said Tum.

'No!' said Jack. 'We have to stop this! *You* have to stop this happening! You're the Marshal!'

'But only in this village. The horsemeat gang operate in a valley outside the village limits. They call it Badlands Valley. There's no law there.'

'But you must be able to catch them!' insisted Milo. 'What about when they come to sell their burgers? You can arrest them then.'

'On what charge?' asked Tum. 'There's no evidence that the horsemeat burgers are made partly from *stolen* horses. They also buy horses legally, and I think they mix the meat from the stolen horses with the legal meat.' He shook his head. 'I'm sorry. I can't touch them.'

'We can!' said Milo vengefully. 'They're not going to take our horse and turn him into burgers! Where is this Badlands Valley?'

'I wouldn't advise going after the gang on your own,' said Tum. 'They're a dangerous bunch. And there are a lot of them. You three wouldn't be any match for them.'

'You'd be surprised how determined we can be when one of our friends is in trouble,' said Jack. Inside, he thought: and hopefully I'll turn into Thud when we meet up with them.

'Okay. If you insist,' shrugged Tum. 'But remember that I've warned you. Turn left at the village hall and follow the main road. When you reach the edge of the village you'll see a road that goes into a valley. There's a sign by it that says: END OF VILLAGE LIMITS. BEYOND THIS POINT IS BADLANDS VALLEY. ENTER AT YOUR OWN RISK.'

'You mean they've got the nerve to put up a sign like that and the law does nothing

24

about it?' said Jack, angry.

'Who does the land belong to?' asked Milo. 'Someone must have control over it!'

'It belongs to a man called Hard Harry. He's the leader of the horsemeat gang. It's his private valley; that's why there's no law there, except Hard Harry's law.'

'Not Hard Harry, the wrestler?' asked Milo.

'He used to be a wrestler,' nodded the Marshal. 'But he retired after he got hurt in a match. He used the money he'd made as a wrestler to buy the valley, and that's when he started his horsemeat business.'

Milo nodded. 'Thank you for your advice, Marshal.' He turned to Big Rock and Jack. 'Okay. Let's go.'

'Wait!' said Jack. 'We can't leave it like this! Our friend is in trouble, and this so-called lawman won't do anything about it!'

'Now listen, you!' growled the Marshal, angrily. 'I'm on my own and I have a hard enough job keeping the law in this village – never mind in Badlands Valley too.'

'We understand, Marshal,' nodded Milo. 'Come on, you two.'

Milo left, with Big Rock following. Jack hesitated, then followed them.

'You gave up very easily!' he snapped accusingly at Milo.

'The Marshal's right. He has no power outside this village. He can't help us. We're going to have to save Robin ourselves. And I think I know a way to do it.'

'How?' demanded Jack.

'We wrestle for him,' said Milo. 'Big Rock against Hard Harry.'

'What makes you think that Hard Harry will take that challenge?' asked Jack. 'You heard what the Marshal said. He retired from wrestling after he got hurt in a match.'

'And the person he was wrestling when he got hurt was Big Rock,' said Milo.

Jack stared at Milo, and then at Big Rock.

'You were the one who injured Hard Harry?' he said.

'Didn't mean to,' said Big Rock sadly. 'Never

want hurt anyone. But Hard Harry cheat. Upset me. I throw him out of ring.'

'And he landed badly,' finished Milo. 'Damaged his leg. I heard he'd stopped wrestling after that, but I didn't know he'd gone into the racket of stealing horses.'

'And sell for burgers,' said Big Rock.

'But if it was Big Rock who finished his wrestling career, what makes you think he'd agree to wrestle Big Rock again, with Robin as the prize?'

'Revenge,' said Milo. 'He'd see this as a way of getting his own back on Big Rock.'

# CHAPTER 3

They returned to the caravan, where they found the Masked Avenger, Meenu and Blaze waiting for them.

'We can't find him,' said the Avenger.

'I flew all over the village, and around it,' said Blaze. 'We don't know where he is.'

'He's in Badlands Valley,' said Jack.

Quickly, they told the others what the Marshal had told them about Hard Harry and his gang of thieves.

'Turning Robin into burgers!' exclaimed Meenu, shocked.

'We can't let that happen!' said the Avenger.

'No, we can't,' said Milo. 'That's why we're going out to Badlands Valley to bargain for Robin.'

'Me wrestle for him,' said Big Rock.

Milo told them about his plan. After he'd finished, they looked at him doubtfully.

'Are you sure it will work?' asked the Avenger.

'No,' admitted Milo. 'But if we don't try, I'm sure that Robin will be turned into burgers.'

'I'll fly on ahead,' offered Blaze. 'I'll try to find Robin, and see what I can do.'

With that, the phoenix flapped his wings and flew away.

'Maybe when we arrive it'll create a distraction so Blaze can get Robin away,' said Jack.

'Unless Robin's already been turned into burgers . . .' sighed Milo.

'Don't talk like that!' snapped Meenu, upset. 'Come on! Let's go!'

They followed the Marshal's directions, turning left at the village hall, then taking the main road out. Once they'd left the built-up area, the road became a rough track. After half an hour of walking, they reached the sign that said, END OF VILLAGE LIMITS. BEYOND THIS

POINT IS BADLANDS VALLEY. ENTER AT YOUR OWN RISK. They walked on, with high rock walls on either side, covered with lichen and weeds. The valley floor was thick with trees and bushes and tall grass.

'Lots of places to hide,' commented Jack.

They walked on for another half an hour, all the time keeping their eyes and ears strained for any sign of Hard Harry's gang, or his hide-out. Suddenly, Big Rock stopped.

'Hear something,' he grunted.

They looked around.

'I can't see anyone,' said Meenu.

'Trolls have got very good hearing,' said Milo. 'If Big Rock says he hears something, he does.'

'What sort of thing?' asked the Masked Avenger.

'Feet,' said Big Rock. 'And click.'

'The kind of click that a crossbow makes when it's being cocked ready for firing?' asked Jack.

'Yes,' nodded Big Rock. 'How you know?'

'Because a man has just come out from behind that tree with one,' said Jack. 'And he's pointing it at us.'

As they looked, more men appeared. Some of them were armed with crossbows, some with spears.

Big Rock let out an angry growl.

'Careful, Big Rock,' warned Milo. 'Starting a fight now won't save Robin.'

The leader of the gang of armed men moved nearer to them, the crossbow in his hands aimed straight at them. He had a big bushy black beard.

'You're trespassing!' he said.

'We've come to see Hard Harry,' said Milo.

The bearded man frowned.

'Why?' he demanded.

'We're old friends of his,' said Milo. 'Old wrestling friends.'

The bearded man stood there, studying them for a while, then he went to join a bald man and they talked briefly in whispers. The bearded man turned back to glare at Milo.

'I recognise him as Big Rock, the Wrestling Troll,' said the bearded man, pointing at Big Rock. 'And she's the Masked Avenger. Who are the rest of you?'

'I'm Milo, the manager of Waldo's Wrestling Trolls,' said Milo. He pointed at Jack and Meenu. 'That's Jack, our assistant trainer. And over there is Meenu, the Masked Avenger's costume maker and dresser.'

'And you're here to see Hard Harry?' queried the bearded man, frowning.

'That's what I said,' replied Milo. 'Is that a problem?'

'It may be for you,' said the bearded man. 'No one ever comes to Badlands Valley looking for Hard Harry, and lives to talk about it.'

# CHAPTER 4

Milo wasn't fazed.

'How about we go and talk to Hard Harry and see what he says?' he replied.

The bearded man and the bald man exchanged doubtful looks, then the bearded man shrugged.

'Might as well,' he grunted. 'You're all gonna die anyway.'

He led the way along the valley track. Jack and the others followed him, with the rest of Hard Harry's armed men bringing up the rear.

'I wonder if Blaze has found Robin yet,' Jack muttered to Milo.

'If so, why hasn't he reappeared?' whispered back Milo.

The valley came to an end as the rocky sides petered out, and they saw that a camp was spread out before them. No, not just a camp; it looked like a small town. It was certainly bigger than the village. There were hundreds of tents and wooden shacks sprawled around.

'There's no sign of any horses,' whispered Meenu.

'Yes there is,' said Jack. He stopped and pointed, and they saw that just outside the camp was a corral, an area surrounded by a high wooden fence. Inside the corral were lots of horses of all different sizes and colours.

'Let's hope Robin's among them,' murmured Milo.

'Get moving!' snapped the bearded man. And he jabbed Milo in the back with the point of his crossbow bolt.

The captives moved on into the camp.

'Well, well, well!' a voice boomed out. 'What have we here?'

They turned to see a very large man limping towards them. His left leg was crooked.

'Trespassers, boss!' said the bearded man. 'They say you know them.'

'I certainly do!' grinned Hard Harry. 'Milo and that big stupid lump of granite – Big Rock.'

'Hello, Harry,' said Milo. 'Long time no see. How are you? How's the leg?'

Hard Harry scowled.

'I'm glad you haven't forgotten that,' he snarled. 'Neither have I.' He frowned, puzzled. 'What are you doing here in my valley?'

'We were in the village for a wrestling tournament,' said Milo. 'The Great Bun Wrestle Smackdown. Big Rock and the Masked Avenger were on the bill.' He gestured towards the Avenger in her red wrestling outfit with a long red cloak and a full-face red mask, which could only be taken off by an opponent if she was beaten in the ring – and so far she was undefeated. 'This is the Masked Avenger.'

'Yes, I've heard of her,' said Harry. He turned to the Masked Avenger. 'I hear you're good.'

'I am,' she replied proudly. 'I'm unbeaten.'

Hard Harry smiled.

'Well, maybe that's about to change,' he smirked. 'I've got a few people in my gang who are pretty good. I reckon they could beat you.'

'Bring them on!' challenged the Masked Avenger.

'Actually, Harry, I'm glad you're still interested in wrestling, because that's why we came to see you,' said Milo. 'You've got a friend of ours. A horse. A talking horse.'

'It's theirs!' exclaimed the bearded man in alarm.

'Shut up, Percy!' snarled Hard Harry. He turned to Milo and demanded: 'Are you accusing me of breaking the law by stealing horses?'

'Well, I'm sure we can ask our horse that question,' said Milo. 'He'll soon tell us.'

'I told you it was dangerous, boss, stealing a talking horse!' said Percy.

'Shut up!' shouted Hard Harry angrily. He turned back to Milo, and now he was grim-faced, unsmiling. 'You're not getting him back,' he said. 'He's gonna be burger meat.'

At these words, Big Rock let out a growl and advanced towards Hard Harry, who limped back from the troll and pushed his men forwards so they stood between him and Big Rock.

'Not a good idea, Big Rock,' said Hard Harry. 'You're outnumbered. My people will bring you down before you get to me.' He looked at Jack and the Masked Avenger. 'And the same goes for the rest of you.'

'Of course it does,' nodded Milo. 'And we wouldn't be so stupid as to try anything like that. But I was thinking, you were always a sporting man.'

'I was,' retorted Harry. He tapped his thigh. 'Until your troll broke my leg!'

'And that's why we thought we'd give you the chance to get your own back,' said Milo. 'Any one of your lot, in a wrestling bout against Big Rock. If your man wins, you keep Robin. If Big Rock wins, we take our horse back.'

Harry regarded Milo and Big Rock thoughtfully. Then he shook his head.

'No,' he said. 'The horse goes for burger meat. But you lot . . . we're going to have to keep you quiet.' He turned to the bearded man. 'Percy!'

'Yes, boss?'

'Kill them.'

# CHAPTER 5

'You can't kill us!' protested Milo, shocked.

'Why not?' demanded Harry.

'Because . . . it wouldn't be fair!'

Harry sneered.

'Fair?' he repeated. 'I was never fair, Milo, and you know that.'

'You cheat,' said Big Rock.

'I do!' said Harry. 'And I'm proud of it! Now, I'm going to check on my burgers. Sorry – horses!' With that, he laughed and walked off.

Percy and some of the other men levelled their crossbows at the gang.

'Sorry about this,' said Percy apologetically. 'But he is the boss. And orders are orders.' He turned to the men. 'Okay, let 'em have it.'

* * *

Hard Harry was almost at the corral where the stolen horses were being held when he saw that there was something wrong. Smoke was coming up from somewhere inside it, and the horses were jumping around. Suddenly one of the fences collapsed, and the horses were running free.

'Stop them!' shouted Harry urgently, and he ran towards the corral as fast as his bad leg would let him.

It was too late. Most of the horses had escaped and were galloping out of the valley, despite the efforts of Harry's men to stop them.

Harry reached the empty corral and grabbed the man nearest to him.

'What happened, Bob?' he demanded.

'It all happened so quick, boss!' said the man. 'This phoenix suddenly flew down and burst into flames and set light to the rope holding part of the fence together. The next second, the fence collapsed and the phoenix suddenly changed into this big horse which galloped out, and all the other horses followed it.'

'A phoenix?' raged Harry.

'I'm sorry, boss,' said the man. 'There was nothing we could do!'

'This is the work of Milo and his gang!' snarled Harry. Then, with a vengeful smile, he added: 'But I've had my own back! They're all dead now!'

'Boss! Boss!'

Harry turned and saw Percy rushing towards him. Percy looked very battered and bruised.

'They got away, boss!'

'Yes, I know,' grunted Harry. 'I saw! All the horses . . . gone!'

'Not the horses. Milo and Big Rock and the others.'

Harry's mouth dropped open in shock and he stared at Percy.

'What?' he said, stunned.

'We were just about to shoot them when this great big troll appeared. I've never seen anything like it! The biggest and strongest troll ever! Before we knew what was happening, he started wading in, punching and throwing us about.' Percy looked as if he was about to cry. 'He hurt me.'

'You idiot! You fool!' stormed Harry. 'You let them get away!'

'It wasn't our fault!' defended Percy. 'It was this giant troll . . .'

'Sound the alarm!' shouted Harry. 'I want them caught! All of them! I want them back here!'

'But what about the giant troll?' asked Percy fearfully.

'You just catch them,' snarled Harry, 'and leave that troll to me!'

# CHAPTER 6

The gang headed away from Hard Harry's camp as quickly as they could.

'We need to go faster!' urged Milo. 'They'll be coming after us!'

'But we haven't got Robin!' burst out Jack.

'I'm hoping Blaze will have seen to that,' said Milo. 'Remember, Jack, you said maybe we'd create a distraction so that Blaze could get Robin away?'

'Which Thud did brilliantly!' Meenu smiled at Jack. 'The way you threw those men around, as if they were just rag dolls!'

'Yes, but that was then,' said the Masked Avenger. 'Now he's Jack again and we're still in danger until we get back to the village.'

From behind a large outcrop of rock they heard the sound of hundreds of horses galloping. They pulled to a halt.

'They find us!' said Big Rock.

'I think we need Thud again!' said Milo to Jack, hopefully.

Suddenly the horses burst into view – but they were all riderless. A large brown horse, leading the herd, veered towards the gang. There was a flash of light, and the large brown horse vanished and was replaced by Blaze.

'Wow!' said the Avenger. 'That was spectacular!'

'You saved the horses, Blaze!' exclaimed Meenu.

'Where Robin?' asked Big Rock, worried.

From behind the rocky outcrop came the plodding sound of hooves, and eventually Robin appeared. He stopped and stood there, out of breath, as the others hurried to him.

'Hurrah!' cried Jack. 'You're safe!'

Meenu and Big Rock rushed to the old horse and hugged him joyously.

'You are so slow!' complained Milo. 'Even when it's a matter of life and death!'

'I'm not used to all this fast galloping,' panted the old horse.

A booming, trumpeting sound echoed along the whole valley.

'That's an alarm!' said Milo. 'Harry's sending everyone after us!'

'Can you see how many of them there are, Blaze?' asked Jack.

The phoenix flapped his wings and soared

into the air. He circled briefly, and then came down to rejoin them.

'There are hundreds of them,' the phoenix said. 'A few are on horseback, most on foot, and they're all armed. They're carrying spears and swords and crossbows. It looks like they're splitting up into different groups, so they can spread out to find us.'

'I think we ought to split up as well,' suggested the Masked Avenger. 'We're a big group and easily spotted. If we split into twos and threes, we might have a better chance.'

'I don't know,' said Jack doubtfully. 'I think we're stronger together. We can back each other up.'

'We can still back each other up,' said Milo. 'So long as we stay near enough that if we run into trouble we can give a shout for help. Then the others can come running.'

'Yes,' nodded the Avenger. 'That's the answer.'

'Okay, Jack?' asked Milo.

'I suppose so,' said Jack reluctantly.

'Right,' said Milo. 'Ava, you and Meenu together. Jack and Robin with Blaze. Me and Big Rock. Let's go!'

The Masked Avenger and Meenu hurried off, making for the rocky wall, keeping to the cover of the rocks and bushes and trees.

'Milo on back!' said Big Rock, and he grabbed hold of Milo and hoisted him up onto his shoulders, then ran off as fast as he could with Milo clinging onto the big troll's neck.

'Good idea,' said Blaze. 'Robin, can you carry Jack?'

Robin stood panting. 'I'll do my best,' he said. 'But I'm still out of breath after all that galloping.'

'Okay, I'll do it,' said Blaze.

There was a flash, and once more the brown horse stood where Blaze had been.

'Let's go!' said Blaze.

Jack climbed up on the horse, which started to gallop off.

'Wait for me!' called Robin.

The brown horse stopped. 'Sorry,' said Blaze.

'Don't worry, Robin,' said Jack. 'We won't leave you. Not now we've got you back.'

Big Rock charged along the road that led out of Badlands Valley, with Milo clinging grimly onto his back as he was shaken about.

'I think we ought to slow down a bit,' suggested Milo. 'We're right in the open and easily seen. Maybe we should creep along quietly, using bushes and trees as cover.'

'No,' said Big Rock. 'We run. No one catch us.'

'Er . . . I think they already have,' said Milo.

Ahead, a group of armed men had appeared from behind some rocks. The men began to form a line across the road.

'I think we're caught, Big Rock,' said Milo unhappily.

'No,' said Big Rock, still running.

The men were now standing in a straight, fixed line and had their spears and swords pointing at the onrushing troll.

'I think –' began Milo again.

*CRASH!! BASH!!*

The big troll busted through the line at speed, sending the men nearest to him tumbling backwards and bowling into the others. Milo turned and looked behind him as Big Rock ran on. Hard Harry's men were lying in a heap or crawling around as they struggled to get up.

'Wow!' said Milo, awed. Then he grinned. 'Go, Big Rock! Keep running!'

The Masked Avenger and Meenu peered out from the entrance of the shallow cave where they'd taken cover.

'I heard something,' said Meenu.

'I heard it, too,' nodded the Avenger. 'It sounded like Milo shouting, "Go, Big Rock! Keep running!"'

'No, there was something else,' said Meenu, frowning. 'A different noise.'

'What sort of noise?' asked the Avenger.

'I don't know.' Meenu shrugged. 'It must have been my imagination. All this business of nearly being killed has made me extra-sensitive.'

'Yes, it does tend to have that effect,' smiled the Avenger. 'Anyway, we'd better get going if we're to keep up with the others.'

She stepped out of the cave with Meenu close behind her. As they did so they heard a noise above them, and they both looked up . . .

# CHAPTER 7

Blaze, in the shape of the large brown horse, with Jack on his back, ran as fast as he could, but he had to stop now and then to let Robin catch up.

'Of course, when I was younger I could go a lot faster than this,' panted the old horse. 'I was known as Galloping Robin.'

Suddenly, Blaze pulled to an abrupt halt.

'What's up?' asked Jack. 'Why have you stopped?'

'I can smell people behind that rock,' said Blaze.

'Maybe it's Milo and Big Rock, or Ava and Meenu,' said Jack.

Blaze shook his head. 'No, I know their scent. This smell is different. These are –'

'Hard Harry's men,' said Robin bitterly, as a gang of armed thugs appeared from their hiding place behind the rock. He looked hopefully at Jack. 'Any chance of you turning into Thud?' he asked. 'Because now would be a very good time.'

Jack willed himself to turn into the giant troll again, doing his best to think troll thoughts, hoping he'd get the sensation of the quartz film over his eyes and feel his body shaking as it began to grow and grow . . . But there was nothing.

'I'm afraid not,' he said.

'Time to dismount, Jack,' said Blaze.

'Trust me, I'm not going to turn into Thud and squash you,' Jack reassured him.

'I'm not worried about you squashing me,' said Blaze. 'But I need to take some action, and I can't do it with you sitting on me.'

'Oh!' said Jack in realisation.

He slipped off the brown horse's back and he and Robin retreated as Hard Harry's men advanced towards them.

There was a flash of light, and where the brown horse had stood there was now a large green dragon. The dragon opened its mouth and let out a burst of fire. When the smoke cleared, they saw Hard Harry's men stumbling about, coughing and choking, smoke rising from their singed clothes. Blaze let fly with another burst of fire, and this time the men threw down their weapons and ran off.

'Nice one, Blaze!' grinned Jack.

'I think I'll keep this shape in case they come back,' said Blaze.

'You'd better fly off,' said Robin. 'You can take Jack with you.'

Jack shook his head.

'No chance,' he said. 'We came here to rescue you, Robin. We're a family. We stay together.' He grinned. 'And if anyone tries to stop us now, I think our dragon will see them off.'

The dragon circled above the field where their caravan was parked, then flew down and landed beside it, changing back into Blaze as Robin trotted into the field, with Jack on his back.

'You didn't have to carry me,' protested Jack. 'I could have run here.'

'Even an old horse like me can run faster than you,' insisted Robin.

The door of the caravan opened and Milo and Big Rock came out.

'You made it!' cried Milo, delighted. 'Great! We've all escaped!'

'Where Ava and Meenu?' asked Big Rock, looking around.

Then the air filled with the sound of hooves and rolling wheels, and they saw Hard Harry and his bearded lieutenant, Percy, approaching them on a large horse-drawn cart. Big Rock

growled and made a move towards the cart as it drew to a halt, but Milo stopped him.

'Wait, Big Rock,' he murmured. 'Let's see what they want first.'

'So, it looks like you nearly got away,' smiled Harry.

'Got away,' grunted Big Rock.

'Not all of you,' said Harry, shaking his head. 'It looks like you're missing a couple. The Masked Avenger and her little friend.' And he smiled. 'We've got them. I'm guessing you'd like them back. So I've come with an offer.'

'I said we should have kept together!' burst out Jack angrily.

'What's your game, Harry?' demanded Milo.

'The same as the one you suggested, Milo,' said Harry. 'Wrestling. With the Masked Avenger and her friend as one of the prizes. One of my gang against one of yours. Yours wins – you all go home safely. Mine wins – the rest of you go, but we keep the horse.'

'How about if we report you to the Marshal?' demanded Milo.

'He can't do anything,' said Harry smugly. 'Your friends are still in my territory in Badlands Valley.'

'Yes, but you're here,' said Milo. 'We could arrest you and take you to him.'

'And he'd have to let me go, because you've got no evidence here,' smirked Harry. 'So, do you want to argue, or do you want your friends back?'

Jack and Milo exchanged looks of anger and frustration.

'How do we even know you've got the Masked Avenger?' demanded Robin.

Harry put his hand in his pocket and pulled out a ring, which he tossed to Milo.

'Take a look at that,' he said. 'Recognise it? That looks like the Royal Crest of the Kingdom of Weevil to me.' He frowned. 'How come a wrestler has a ring like that?'

Milo showed the ring to Big Rock, Robin, Jack and Blaze, who all nodded unhappily.

'She was . . . er . . . she was given it by the ruler of Weevil for services to the Kingdom,' said Milo.

'Was she indeed? So, do you take my challenge?'

'No!' said Jack. 'You're not to be trusted!'

Harry sighed.

'That's a pity,' he said. 'Well, I guess we'll just have to kill the pair of them.'

There was a low growl, and the next second Big Rock, moving with surprising speed, had dragged Harry from the cart and was holding him off the ground with one huge hand, his other fist pulled back ready to punch.

'No!' snarled Big Rock. '*You* die!'

'Killing me isn't a good idea, Big Rock,' said Harry calmly. 'I've left instructions that if Percy and I don't arrive back in an hour, the girls die.'

'You lie!' snapped Big Rock.

'Want to put it to the test?' asked Harry.

'Let him go, Big Rock,' said Milo sadly.

Big Rock hesitated, then he let go of Harry. Harry fell to the ground, got up and dusted himself off.

'Percy and I will give you time to talk it over. You've got ten minutes, then we head back.'

With that, Harry climbed back on the cart and he and Percy drove it to the other side of the field. The gang waited for them to move out of earshot, and then turned hastily to one another.

'I don't like it,' said Jack. 'Why is Harry making the very same offer that he turned down when you made it to him?'

'Because he's got some kind of secret plan, of course,' said Robin. 'He's going to double-cross us.'

Milo shook his head.

'But how? He must know that we'll tell the Marshal everything, and if anything happens to us in Badlands Valley, the Marshal could send for the Rangers.'

'If that's the case, why hasn't the Marshal sent for the Rangers before?' demanded Jack.

'Because before it's just been about stealing horses and turning them into burgers,' said Milo. 'Killing people is more serious.'

'Excuse me!' snorted Robin indignantly. 'Not to a horse, it isn't!'

'Yes, sorry, Robin,' apologised Milo. 'I didn't mean to be rude . . .'

'Well it *was* rude!' said the old horse. 'How would you like it if I said that horses were more important than people?'

'Well . . .' said Milo awkwardly.

'Or money more important than rock,' put in Big Rock.

Milo turned to look at the big troll, puzzled. 'Money *is* more important than rocks,' he said.

'Not to a troll,' said Jack.

Milo groaned. 'Look, we're getting off the point!' he said. 'What are we going to do about Princess Ava and Meenu?'

'We do what Harry says,' said Robin.

'We can't,' said Jack, shaking his head. 'Harry is going to cheat in some way, so we'll lose the match. Which means you'll be turned into burger meat. And there's no guarantee that Harry will keep his word about letting any of us go! He might just kill us all and not even bother with a wrestling match!'

'Hard Harry cheat!' agreed Big Rock.

'Exactly!' said Jack.

'Right now, Princess Ava and Meenu are in serious danger,' said Robin firmly. 'We've got to do everything we can to rescue them. It's what we do. We're a family. We stick together. And if it means I end up in big trouble, so be it.'

Milo looked thoughtful for a moment. 'Not necessarily,' he said.

The others looked at him, curious.

# CHAPTER 8

The large cart rolled into Badlands Valley and pulled to a halt by Hard Harry's camp.

'Out you get!' said Harry.

Jack, Milo and Big Rock got down from the back of the cart. Robin, who had been walking alongside the vehicle as they travelled, looked around the camp.

'I don't see any sign of the Masked Avenger or Meenu,' he whispered.

'You will,' said a voice, and they turned to look into Harry's smiling face.

'Do you always listen in on other people's conversations?' demanded Robin sniffily.

'Only when I'm going to eat them,' winked Harry. He gave a shrill whistle, and the flap of a tent opened and the Masked Avenger and Meenu were pushed out. They were tied together by a piece of thick rope around their ankles, so they couldn't escape.

'Time for you old friends to catch up,' grinned Harry. 'I'll go and set up the ring for the match.'

He gestured at his men, who were standing around, watching them, glaring angrily.

'I wouldn't try any funny business,' said Harry. 'My people would like their revenge for what you did to them, and that would give them an excuse.'

'We could beat all of your people with both hands tied behind our backs!' said Milo defiantly.

'Maybe we ought to tie your legs together as well,' laughed Harry. Then, still chuckling, he walked off.

As soon as he had gone, the Avenger turned angrily on the gang.

'You idiots!' she raged. 'We could have got out of here! Now, with you here, we're in worse trouble!'

'We came here to save you!' protested Jack.

'Yes? Well you're not doing a very good job of it!'

'Some people are never grateful!' huffed Robin.

'Let's not argue among ourselves,' urged Milo. 'Let's get our plan of action worked out. First, we've got to find out what Hard Harry is *really* up to. Why did he drag us back here?'

'We can tell you that!' snapped the Avenger. 'He wants Thud.'

'What?' said Milo, surprised. 'How do you know?'

'These things called ears,' said the Avenger sarcastically, pointing to her own. 'We heard him talking to his man, Percy.'

Meenu added, 'Harry was so impressed with what Thud did to his men that he said, "I have to get hold of that Wrestling Troll! I could make a fortune from him!"'

'But he brought *us* here, not Thud,' said Robin, bewildered. Then a look of shocked realisation came into his face and he said, 'Unless he knows about Jack . . .'

Meenu shook her head.

'No,' she said. 'At least, we don't think so. What he said was, "He appeared out of nowhere and came to their rescue when they were in trouble. So, we'll put them in trouble again, and when he appears, we'll trap him!"'

'How trap?' asked Big Rock.

'We don't know,' the Avenger admitted. 'They went off and we didn't hear any more.'

They heard heavy footsteps approaching, and then Hard Harry returned.

'Okay,' he said. 'Everything's ready. Follow me.'

The gang followed Hard Harry to where a wrestling ring had been put up in a large open space that was bordered by tall trees. A huge man was waiting in the ring. He was very, *very* tall, with a shaved head and muscular arms so thick they looked like legs. And his legs, in turn, looked like . . . well, thick tree trunks.

'Wow!' said Milo. 'He's big!'

'This is Chuck,' said Hard Harry. 'He used to wrestle with me in the old days. Then he was known as Mr Mysterious.' He grinned at the

Masked Avenger. 'He did your trick. He wore a full-face mask, and he'd only take it off if he was beaten.'

'I remember him!' said Milo. 'I saw him wrestle when my Uncle Waldo was in charge of Waldo's Wrestling Trolls. He was nasty! A cheat! A dirty wrestler!'

'Thank you,' smiled Hard Harry. 'Chuck will be flattered.'

'Who beat him?' asked Jack. 'After all, he's not wearing his mask now.'

'Chuck doesn't need to wear a mask any more,' said Harry. 'Everyone in Badlands Valley knows who he is.'

'Now we do too,' said Big Rock.

'Yes,' smiled Harry.

'Harry's going to kill us,' snapped the Avenger angrily. 'After the match is over. That's why he doesn't care if we see Chuck without his mask!'

'No, no, miss,' said Hard Harry reprovingly. 'I meant what I said. If your wrestler loses, I keep the horse, but the rest of you go away safely. If Chuck loses, you all get to go.'

With that, Harry went to join Chuck.

'Whatever he says, I don't trust him,' said the Avenger. 'He's got some trick up his sleeve.'

'Of course he has,' agreed Milo.

'Okay!' called Hard Harry. 'Let's get this bout under way!'

'Here come!' grunted Big Rock, and he took hold of the ropes and began to climb into the ring.

'Not you, Big Rock,' said Harry. He pointed at Jack. 'Him.'

They stared at Hard Harry.

'But Jack's not a wrestler!' Milo protested.

'Good,' said Harry. 'Then Chuck should finish him off easily.'

'This is cheating!' burst out the Avenger.

'Refuse to fight, Jack,' said Meenu.

'I can't,' said Jack. 'If I do, his man will win by default.'

'But take a look above the ring!' whispered Meenu urgently. 'Hanging from the trees.'

They did, and saw that a huge net made of metal had been suspended from the branches of the trees directly above the ring.

'So that's his plan,' said Milo. 'Jack's the bait. When he gets battered in the ring, they expect that Thud will come to help, and they'll drop that net, trapping him.'

'So it's very important that you don't change,' muttered the Masked Avenger to Jack.

'But I can't control it!' Jack pointed out.

'Come on!' barked Hard Harry. 'My man's waiting!'

'Give in quickly,' urged Milo. 'That way you won't get hurt.'

Jack shook his head.

'No,' he said firmly. 'If I do, Hard Harry wins. And besides, I've still got a chance. Chuck may be stronger than me, but I've got wrestling skills. I'll use them against him.' He grinned. 'I can win this!'

Jack climbed through the ropes into the ring and went to his corner.

# CHAPTER 9

Hard Harry limped to the centre of the ring.

'And now, the Great Badlands Valley Wrestling Challenge! In one corner, our very own champion, Chuck. In the other corner, the challenger, Jack!'

The large crowd of men shouted and cheered when Chuck's name was called out, and laughed in derision when Harry announced Jack.

As Harry climbed out of the ring, Milo protested: 'You haven't said about the rules!'

'No rules,' said Harry. 'Winner wins. Loser loses. First one who gets two pinfalls or a knockout is the winner. Begin!'

Jack moved warily to the centre of the ring, his eyes on Chuck. His opponent was big and tough, but that didn't mean that he couldn't beat him. I have the knowledge, thought Jack. I know about wrestling holds. I know about throws. All I have to do is . . .

*GRAB!*

The next second, Chuck grabbed Jack round the neck with one hand, his other huge hand taking hold of one of Jack's knees, and then . . .

*BANG!*

Jack found himself crashing down onto the ground with such force that it drove all the air out of him.

*CRUNCH!*

The heavy body of Chuck fell on Jack with all his weight. Jack struggled to lift his shoulders off the ground – even one shoulder – but it was no good.

'One! Two! Three!' shouted Hard Harry triumphantly. 'First pinfall to Chuck!'

Hard Harry's gang cheered and laughed as Jack forced himself to his feet.

'You're doing okay, Jack!' called Milo encouragingly.

'I'm glad you think so,' said Jack unhappily.

Once again, Chuck reached out a huge hand to grab hold of Jack, but this time Jack swayed back out of reach. Chuck advanced, his legs bent and his arms spread wide, an evil smile on his face. Jack darted forward, and then dropped and slid between Chuck's legs, jumping up behind him. Before Chuck could turn round, Jack had rushed at Chuck's back, and then climbed up it and wrapped his legs around Chuck's thick neck.

'*Yes!*' yelled Milo excitedly. 'Fantastic!'

'Go, Jack, go!' shouted the Avenger.

Jack took hold of Chuck's face and leaned back, trying to pull his opponent backwards. But Chuck was very strong. The wrestler bent forward, bringing Jack with him, at the same time reaching round behind him and catching hold of Jack by his head.

As Jack struggled to keep his grip on Chuck's head, he could feel a dizziness coming over him. He was aware that his eyes were starting to go filmy and he felt his arms and legs begin to ache, and then grow . . .

Oh no, he thought. Not now! This is exactly what Hard Harry wants!

But just then the feelings vanished and he was flying through the air, aware that he was hurtling out of the ring, thrown by Chuck.

*CRASH!!!!*

Jack crashed into the hard ground with a force that shook him right through his body. His ribs hurt. His head hurt. His whole body hurt.

He was aware of Milo, Big Rock, the Masked Avenger and Meenu kneeling beside him, looking at him anxiously.

'How do you feel?' asked Milo.

'I feel like I've been bashed up and thrown out of a wrestling ring,' groaned Jack. 'I hurt.'

'And the winner, by a knockout, is Chuck!' boomed Hard Harry. 'Take the horse!'

As Percy took hold of Robin's reins, Big Rock lumbered towards them.

'No!' he shouted angrily.

Milo hurried after the big troll and grabbed hold of him. 'Don't worry, Big Rock,' he whispered. 'It's under control!'

'They eat Robin!' shouted Big Rock, distraught.

Milo noticed that Harry had moved within earshot, so aloud he said: 'Yes! But he gave his life for us! He was a true friend!'

'Robin my friend!' moaned Big Rock. 'I not leave him!'

'We have to, Big Rock!' said Milo loudly. Then he leant towards the very unhappy troll and whispered, 'It's going to be all right. But . . . sssh! I'll tell you about it later.'

With that, Milo turned to Harry.

'Well, Harry. You won fair and square. And I hope you're going to keep your word about letting the rest of us go.'

'Of course,' growled Harry. But Milo noticed that Harry didn't look happy at the victory – he kept looking around, searching for something.

He's looking for Thud, realised Milo. This was all about capturing Thud, and it didn't happen.

Harry limped over to his bearded lieutenant.

'Percy, put them in the cart and take them back to the village.' Then, as Percy was about to walk towards the cart, Harry grabbed his lieutenant and whispered something in his ear before letting him move off.

The Masked Avenger had left Meenu to look after Jack and now she joined Milo. She gestured at Harry and Percy.

'What was all that about?' she asked suspiciously.

'Something sneaky, I bet,' said Milo.

'Come on!' shouted Percy. 'Get in the cart!'

'Get in the cart, Big Rock,' said Milo.

'But Robin . . .!' moaned the troll.

'In the cart,' said Milo firmly.

Big Rock clambered onto the back of the cart, looked at Robin as the old horse was tied to a post, and burst into tears.

'You're not really going to leave Robin with them, are you?' asked the Avenger.

'Ssssh,' said Milo. 'I'll explain later.'

The Avenger looked at Meenu, who was still kneeling beside the fallen Jack, gently dabbing at his bruises with a damp cloth.

'We'd better give Meenu a hand to carry Jack,' she said.

They walked over, just as Meenu was helping Jack get to his feet.

'How is he?' asked Milo.

'Bruised but okay,' said Meenu. 'You were very brave, Jack.'

'Yes,' agreed Jack. 'But it hurt.' He gestured for the others to move in closer, then he said, 'I heard what Harry whispered to Percy.'

'How?' asked Meenu, puzzled. 'I was here with you and I didn't hear what he said.'

'I guess it's because I'm part troll,' said Jack. 'Trolls have good hearing.'

'What did he say?' asked Milo.

'He said, "We've got to make that giant troll appear. When you're on the road, go to kill them. That might do it." Then Percy said, "What if the giant troll doesn't come?" and Harry said, "Kill them anyway."'

'They're going to kill us after all!' said Meenu, shocked.

'I expected something like that,' said Milo grimly. 'Hard Harry always did cheat and lie.'

'And you've got a plan to save us?' asked the Avenger eagerly.

'Us? Er . . . no,' admitted Milo.

The Avenger stared at him.

'You haven't?' she said, aghast. 'You came all the way here, knowing the evil sort of person Hard Harry is, putting us all in danger, and you didn't have a plan?'

'You were already in danger!' protested Milo. 'We came here to save you!'

'Come on, you lot!' shouted Percy impatiently.

'Stop jabbering and get in the cart!'

'Okay,' whispered Milo. 'I've got a plan. I'm calling it Plan A. Once we're on our way, we push the driver off the seat, grab the reins and head for the village as fast as we can.'

'You call that a plan?' scoffed the Avenger.

'You got a better idea?' demanded Milo.

'No,' she admitted.

'Then that's what we'll do.'

Milo, the Masked Avenger, Meenu and Jack got to the cart and climbed in. Jack sat next to Big Rock, who was still crying quietly.

'Don't cry, Big Rock,' whispered Jack. 'Robin's okay.'

'No,' sobbed Big Rock. 'He turn into burgers.'

As the cart jolted forward and began to move off, accompanied by Hard Harry's gang, Big Rock looked to where the old horse was tethered and sobbed again.

'That's not Robin,' whispered Jack. 'That's Blaze.'

Bewildered, the big troll turned to Jack and said, 'What?'

'Remember that trick we used before, when I was in prison and Blaze took the shape of Robin so I could get out?'

Big Rock nodded.

'Well, we used that trick again. We left Robin inside the caravan. Blaze did the switch when your back was turned. Once we're safe, Blaze will turn back into his phoenix shape and fly away to safety.'

'Why you no tell me?' demanded Big Rock angrily.

'Ssssh!' urged Jack, shooting a look at Percy, who was driving the cart. But Percy seemed to be busy keeping the cart on the track, and didn't appear to be listening to what they were saying.

'Milo was worried that you might say something and give the game away,' whispered Jack.

The big troll glared at Milo.

Milo frowned. 'What?' he asked.

'Jack tell me about Robin –' said Big Rock angrily, before Jack slapped a hand over the big troll's mouth to silence him.

'Ssssh!' he said urgently.

'It not fair,' glowered Big Rock. 'I not thick! I got brain!'

'Yes, but . . .' Jack faltered. 'Sometimes you say things without thinking. And we needed this to be a secret.'

'Then why tell me now?' demanded Big Rock, still annoyed.

'Because we've found out they're going to kill us all.'

'They kill us?' shouted Big Rock in a loud voice, shocked.

The cart pulled to a halt and Percy turned round to look at them in alarm.

'They know!' he yelled to the rest of his men.

'Well, I think that's another secret out of the bag,' groaned Milo.

'Kill them!' shouted Percy to the other gang members.

# CHAPTER 10

'Okay. Plan A!' shouted Milo. 'Big Rock, throw the driver off!'

Before Percy realised what was happening, Big Rock had grabbed him and hurled him off the cart into a thorny bush.

'Ow!' yelled Percy.

The rest of Hard Harry's gang rushed at the cart and began to climb on, waving their swords and spears. Big Rock, Jack, the Avenger and Meenu did their best to keep the invaders at bay, while Milo leapt into the driver's seat, snatched up the reins and shouted 'Go!' to the horse.

'No,' said the horse. 'If I do, Hard Harry will turn me into burgers!'

'It's another talking horse!' said Meenu in surprise.

'We won't let Harry get you. Not if we get away!' pleaded Milo. 'I promise you, you'll have your freedom!'

'I don't know,' said the horse doubtfully.

'Hurry up and get this cart moving!' shouted the Avenger. 'We're being outnumbered!'

More and more of Hard Harry's gang were scrambling to climb on board. As fast as Big Rock and the others let fly with punches and knocked them off, more took their places.

'*Please!*' Milo begged the horse.

The horse's ears pricked up.

'The magic word!' it said. 'No one's said that to me in years! Right, hold on!'

And with that, the horse leapt forward, jerking the cart so that Harry's gang members fell off onto the ground. Milo, Big Rock, Jack, the Avenger and Meenu nearly toppled out as well, but they just managed to regain their balance and hold on.

'Go!' yelled Milo at the horse. 'Please, please, please, go!'

Hard Harry stood beside the old horse he thought was Robin and smiled as he heard the shouting coming from a short distance away.

'You know what that is?' he asked. 'That is the sound of my people killing your friends.'

And he laughed.

'You mean you broke your word?' said Blaze/Robin. 'You broke the promise you made?'

'Of course!' laughed Hard Harry. 'Milo should have known I would! He knows what I'm like!'

'A cheat and a liar,' said the old horse.

'Exactly,' nodded Harry. 'And a *hungry* cheat and a liar who likes horse meat!'

'Boss! Boss!'

Harry turned and saw Percy running towards him, waving his arms in panic.

'Boss! They did it again! They got away!'

Immediately, Harry was alert. 'You mean that giant troll appeared again and saved them?'

'No. They attacked us.' And he gave an unhappy cry as he added, 'They threw me into a thorny bush. It hurt.'

Harry scowled. He pulled out a sword and glared at Robin.

'Okay. I was going to do this later, but doing it now will make me happy!'

He raised the sword and swung it at Robin but, before the blade could make contact with the old horse, there was a flash of light, and the blade just went through empty air.

'Yes, that's something we didn't tell you about,' said a voice above Harry.

Harry looked up in astonishment and saw the phoenix hovering over him.

'Bye,' said Blaze, and flew off.

'Aaaarghhhh!' roared Harry. He turned to Percy. 'Bring me the fastest horses we've got left, and as many men as you can! We're going after them! I can't trust you idiots to do anything right! I shall do this myself!'

# CHAPTER 11

The cart leapt and jumped as it rattled along the valley track. Jack and the others clung to the sides to stop themselves being thrown out. Suddenly the Masked Avenger gave a cry of alarm.

'Look!' she shouted.

They looked. Behind them were riders, galloping fast. At the front was Hard Harry himself.

'They're gaining on us!' called Meenu to Milo. 'Can't we go any faster?'

'I'm going as fast as I can!' panted the horse. 'It's all right for them, they're just horses with one man on their backs. I'm pulling a cart with a lot of heavy people on it.'

'Me get off!' said Big Rock.

And he leapt off the back of the cart, fell over, then got up and stood ready, fists bunched.

'We can't leave Big Rock!' said Jack, and he, too, jumped off the cart and joined the troll. The Avenger and Meenu had also leapt off the moving cart and gone to stand with Big Rock.

Milo pulled the horse and cart to a halt. 'What's going on?' he demanded.

'I'm calling this Plan B!' shouted back the Masked Avenger.

'It's what friends do,' said Jack. 'One for all and all for one!'

'Yes,' agreed Milo with a sigh, and he got down off the driver's seat and joined his friends.

'Well, I'm not staying!' said the horse. 'If Hard Harry catches me, I'll be in trouble. And a pie!'

With that the horse galloped off, taking the cart with it.

By now, Hard Harry and his gang were almost upon them. Then came the sound of wings beating, and a shadow fell over them. Jack

looked up and his face broke into a grin as he
saw a large green dragon swooping down.

'Blaze!' he cried.

*THUNK!*

Jack's smile changed to a look of horror as
he saw a spear hit the dragon and thud into its
body. The dragon tumbled out of the sky and
crashed to the ground.

'No!' yelled Jack in anguish.

'Get them!' roared Hard Harry.

Jack looked towards the voice. Hard Harry and Percy and the rest of his gang were almost on them now, swords and spears waving. An overwhelming feeling of anger and outrage filled Jack. They had been cheated and lied to, abused and beaten, and now their best friend, Blaze the phoenix, had been brutally and savagely killed!

Jack's eyes filled with tears. No, not tears. These were harder than tears. It was as if there was a sort of thick glass over his eyes, a film of silica . . .

'*GRAAARRRRR!!!!!*'

Milo heard the roar and looked round, and his face split into a grin as he saw the massive figure of Thud towering over him.

'*Yesss!*' enthused Milo.

Hard Harry had pulled his horse to a halt and was staring up at the huge creature with a look of shock and horror on his face.

'That's the one, boss!' said Percy in alarm.

As Thud advanced on the gang, Hard Harry gulped and wheeled his horse round.

'Run!' he yelled.

*CRUNCH!*

Before he could move, one of Thud's enormous hands had swooped down and grabbed hold of Hard Harry, and flung him head first to the ground with a force that shook the earth.

Hard Harry let out a groan and tried to push himself up, but fell over, unconscious.

'GRAAARRRRR!!!!' roared Thud again.

'Run!' yelled Percy in a panic.

Hard Harry's gang turned their horses round and galloped back towards their camp as fast as they could.

'Wow!' said Meenu.

'No chance to bash 'em!' snorted Big Rock, watching the retreating gang.

'I'm not complaining,' said Milo in relieved tones.

The sound of galloping hooves and rumbling wheels approaching fast made them turn. The horse and cart were returning, with Robin running along behind.

'You didn't think I was going to stay out of this!' said Robin.

'He persuaded me that coming back was the right thing to do,' said the other horse. 'He said that if we were united we could beat the crooks!'

'Yes!' said Robin. 'Let me at them! Where are they?'

'They've gone,' said the Masked Avenger.

'Gone?'

'Retreated. Run away.'

'You mean I galloped all the way back here for nothing?' burst out the old horse angrily. 'What made them go?'

'Thud,' said Milo.

Robin looked at Jack, who had turned back into himself again and stood looking dazed.

Jack looked at the crumpled body of the dragon, with the spear still sticking out of it.

'They killed Blaze!' he said, and now he began to cry, but real tears this time, not the hard, angry tears that had come when he'd turned into Thud.

'No, you idiot!' shouted the Masked Avenger.

She ran to the dragon, took hold of the spear and tugged at it, pulling it out of the dragon's body.

As soon as the spear was removed, the dragon disappeared in a dazzling ball of flame. As the flame died down they saw Blaze getting to his feet and flexing his wings.

'Now that was odd!' said Blaze. 'I don't think I've ever been killed before. Although I may have been, I suppose. It's not something you remember.'

'He's a phoenix!' said the Avenger impatiently. 'They regenerate, as well as change shape. When they die they burst into flames and come back to life, all new and strong again!'

'I knew that,' said Big Rock.

'Yes, all right. I suppose I did, too,' said Jack. 'It was just . . . seeing that spear hit the dragon.'

Meenu pointed at the unconscious Hard Harry.

'I think it would be a good time to put an end to Hard Harry and his horse-stealing racket,' she said. 'And I think I know how to do it.'

# CHAPTER 12

Hard Harry sat in the Village Marshal's office and looked, in desperate appeal, across the desk to the puzzled Marshal Tom Tum.

'Now let me get this straight,' said Tum. 'You are confessing to stealing horses and you want me to make sure you go to trial and are locked up.'

'Yes.' Hard Harry nodded energetically.

'Why?' asked Tum.

Hard Harry cast a fearful look out of the window.

'Because there's this giant troll out there, and they say that if I don't confess, he'll come and get me.' He shuddered. 'I've never seen anything so terrifying in my life!'

'But what about the rest of your gang?' queried Marshal Tum.

'They've gone,' said Hard Harry. 'They've quit a life of crime. That giant troll has scared us all into going straight.' He shuddered at the memory of Thud. 'And as for the horses, they've all gone too. They've been turned loose.'

Tum shook his head.

'This is one of the strangest things I've ever heard,' he said. He pulled a form towards him and began to fill it in. In the space where it said *Name of accused*, he wrote: *Hard Harry. Confessed.*

The caravan with WWT on the side trundled along the road out of Bun. Milo and Jack were on the driving seat, with Ava and Meenu sitting on the roof. Big Rock ran round and round the moving caravan, practising wrestling kicks as he did so, and Blaze flew overhead in lazy loops.

'This caravan is so heavy!' complained Robin.

'We could all get off if you like,' offered Jack. 'That'd make it lighter.'

'If you did that, who'd be driving it?' demanded Robin.

'You don't need a driver,' said Ava. 'You know where you're going.'

'What he means is, he wouldn't have anything to moan about,' grinned Meenu.

'What happened to the other horse?' asked Jack. 'The one who talked?'

'We had a chat and he decided to go off on his own,' said Robin.

'That's a pity,' said Milo. 'He would have been company for you.'

'I've got all the company I need right here,' said Robin. There was a pause, and then he added: 'Anyway, I like being special – which means there's only room for one talking horse in this family.'

And with that the old horse broke into song as he trudged along:

'Wrestling Trolls,
Tum-di-dum!'

And Jack, Milo, Ava, Meenu, Big Rock and Blaze all joined in:

'Wrestling Trolls,
Tum-di-dum!'

# FAMILY HEIRLOOM

# CHAPTER 1

Jack sat on the steps of the Waldo's Wrestling Trolls caravan and sewed yet another patch over a hole in Big Rock's wrestling costume.

'You need a new outfit, Big Rock,' he said. 'This isn't even a costume any more, it's just a load of patches sewn together.'

'That my lucky costume,' said Big Rock.

'But say it falls apart when you're in the middle of a bout?' argued Jack. 'You'd have nothing on. Everyone would see you naked.'

'I put pants on, in case,' said Big Rock.

Sometimes, thought Jack, there was no use in arguing with Big Rock. He was as stubborn as . . . well, as a rock.

Right now he was standing rigid and letting

Robin, the old horse, push against him to try to knock him over, as a way of improving his balance in the wrestling ring. From the look of fed-up-ness on Robin's face, and the groaning and panting coming from him, the old horse wasn't enjoying the exercise.

'Push harder!' said Big Rock.

'I am pushing harder!' snorted Robin, and he put his head down and pushed with all his weight against the troll. Big Rock remained exactly where he was.

Milo appeared from inside the caravan and looked towards the troll and the old horse.

'How are they doing?' he asked.

'Robin's fed up,' said Jack.

They heard the sound of wings flapping loudly above them, and they looked up as Blaze the phoenix came hurtling down out of the sky and skidded to a halt on the roof of the caravan, grabbing with his claws to stop himself sliding off.

'Careful, Blaze!' said Milo. 'You could hurt yourself coming in as fast as that.'

'Something's happened!' said the phoenix.

'What?' asked Jack.

'Lord Veto's disappeared!'

Jack and Milo exchanged puzzled looks.

'What do you mean, disappeared?' asked Jack.

'Just that,' answered Blaze. 'He's vanished. Gone. Him and Warg, his Chief Orc, have left Veto Castle. And no one knows where they are.'

Big Rock and Robin joined them, brought over by the raised voices.

'What's that about Lord Veto?' asked Robin.

'Blaze says he's disappeared!' repeated Milo.

Jack shook his head. 'No. He's just gone off somewhere with his wrestlers for a tournament, or for some sneaky and crooked scam. He does it all the time.'

'Not in this case,' said Blaze. 'They're saying that he owed money to lots of people, and he can't pay. So he's run away,' added Blaze. 'Now Veto Castle is going to be sold at auction, along with everything in it, to clear his debts.'

Jack looked worried.

'When's the auction taking place?' he asked.

'Tomorrow,' said Blaze.

'Then I have to go there right now,' said Jack. 'There's something I have to get hold of before the place is sold and the new owners move in.'

'What?' asked Big Rock.

'It's to do with my parents.'

'You've never told us about your parents,' said Milo. 'Who were they?'

'I don't know,' admitted Jack. 'Lord Veto told me they worked for him and died in an accident when I was just a year old. He said he kept me on out of kindness.'

'That doesn't sound like Lord Veto . . .' said Robin.

'No,' agreed Jack. 'And he wasn't kind at all. He was harsh and cruel to me, and to everyone who worked for him. I started as a kitchen boy for him when I was four years old, and was there for six years, right up to the time when he threw me out. If you hadn't come to my rescue that night, I don't know what would have happened to me.'

'If you didn't know your parents, how do you know there's something to do with them inside Veto Castle?' asked Milo.

'They left me a ring,' said Jack. 'My mother sewed it to my baby clothes. One of the kitchen women, who used to help take care of me after my mother died, told me she'd done it so it wouldn't get lost. She also told me if Lord Veto found out about it, he'd throw it away. So I hid it behind a brick in the wall next to my sleeping basket in the kitchen. If I'd known

Lord Veto was going to throw me out, I'd have taken it with me.' He sighed. 'If someone buys Veto Castle and starts knocking down walls, they'll find it and take it. Either that, or it will be lost for ever. I have to get it back before that happens!'

# CHAPTER 2

As they drew near to Veto Castle, they could see what looked like a camp set up in the grounds, with caravans and tents sprawling around beneath the high walls of the old fortress. A big board had been put up next to the main gateway: FOR SALE BY AUCTION. EVERYTHING MUST GO.

'Looks like everyone's here to try to get a bargain,' said Milo.

Robin pulled the Wrestling Trolls caravan through the open gates and they found a place to park, away from the rest of the camp. The crowd seemed to be mainly humans, though there was a large contingent of goblins and a few orcs were strutting around scowling at everyone.

'They look like Lord Veto's orcs,' said Jack.

'I expect they're here hoping to get hold of their wages,' said Robin. 'I bet Lord Veto owes them money.'

'Lord Veto owes everyone money!' snapped an elf who'd appeared beside them. 'He owes me a hundred gold coins for work I did for him! If you're here to get money, you'll have to wait in the queue.'

'No, we're here for the auction,' said Milo. 'We've come to look at the stuff that's for sale. See if there are any bargains.'

'You'll have to wait until

tomorrow,' said the elf. 'The castle's being locked up until then. They're worried that people will take stuff away in payment for what they're owed. That's why we elves have demanded the local guards come here to make sure no one gets in before then. There are lots of angry people here and we'll need protection if things get rough.'

With that, the elf went off.

'It looks like Lord Veto has upset a lot of folks,' commented Blaze.

As they looked around the camp, they saw that many people did indeed appear to be very angry. There were arguments going on, raised voices and fingers being pointed accusingly.

'This is a dangerous situation,' observed Milo. 'With the place locked up, and everyone watching everyone else suspiciously, I don't know how we're going to get in and find this ring of yours, Jack.'

Jack looked around to make sure he couldn't be overheard, then he whispered, 'I know a secret way into the castle. Remember, I lived here all my life. There's a tunnel. The entrance is a hole near the riverbank. Lord Veto's grandfather had the tunnel dug so he could get away if the castle was attacked.'

'Yo! Guys!'

The cheery shout made them turn, and they saw Princess Ava and Meenu heading towards them.

'Princess!' smiled Milo. 'What are you doing here?'

'When I heard about the auction, I had to come along and see it for myself,' said Ava.

'Veto Castle, up for sale! I can't believe it! What about you?'

'Jack's here for something precious,' whispered Milo.

Quickly, Jack explained to Ava and Meenu about trying to find the ring he'd hidden inside the castle kitchen.

'Hey, count us in!' offered Ava eagerly. 'Right, Meenu?'

'Absolutely!' agreed Meenu.

'Although it's not going to be easy,' added Ava, her face suddenly concerned. 'Have you heard who's selling Veto Castle?'

'No,' said Jack. 'Who?'

Princess Ava looked around to make sure that no one was in earshot, then she whispered, 'The Voyadis. They took it when Veto couldn't pay them what he owed.'

'Wow!' exclaimed Milo. 'If Lord Veto owes *them* money and can't pay, it's no wonder he's run away.'

'Who Voyadis?' asked Big Rock.

'They are a *very* powerful and *very* rich

family,' said Princess Ava. 'But they're also very secret. The chief of the clan is called King Voyadi, but most of the others are shadowy figures who are rarely seen. They prefer to stay out of the public eye.'

'King?' said Jack. 'So they're royalty?'

'No,' said Ava. 'But they own royalty. In fact, they own lots of different kingdoms. What they do is lend money to royal families and people with castles and land.'

'Like Lord Veto.'

'Right,' nodded Ava. 'When my father was King of Weevil and we were struggling for money, the Voyadis offered to lend him what the country needed. But when my father worked out how much he'd have to pay back, he said no. They charge lots of interest on the money they lend. So if you borrow a hundred gold coins, you have to pay a hundred gold coins every year for as long as you've borrowed the money.'

Milo did a quick calculation.

'So if you borrowed a hundred gold coins

from them for five years, you'd have to pay back five hundred gold coins.'

'Plus the original hundred you borrowed,' said Ava. 'And the longer you don't pay, the more you owe them. And because the Voyadis are clever, what happens is they suddenly turn up and demand all the money they're owed. And if you can't pay them, they take things in place of payment. Castles. Land. In some cases, whole kingdoms.'

'That *is* clever,' said Robin. Then, as the others looked at him in disapproval, he added quickly, 'But very wrong. Clever, but wrong.'

'So these Voyadis must have turned up here and demanded that Lord Veto pay them the money he owes them,' finished Ava.

'But I don't understand why Lord Veto would run off,' said Jack. 'I've never known him to be afraid of anyone. He's a nasty bully who's got his Wrestling Orcs to protect him.'

'That may be,' said Ava, 'but the Voyadis are *really* dangerous. They have an army of deadly creatures working for them.'

'What sort of deadly creatures?' asked Robin.

'All sorts. Monsters. But the most dangerous are the ninjas. They're deadly assassins who can move without being seen. People say they are so terrifying that even orcs are scared of them. So I guess that's why Lord Veto ran away.'

'In that case, I'm glad we're not going to have anything to do with these Voyadis,' shuddered Robin.

'Nothing to do with them . . . except to get into Veto Castle and get my ring back before the auction,' said Jack.

'That'll be a problem,' said Ava, frowning. 'The Voyadis won't allow it!'

'They not know,' said Big Rock. 'Jack know way in.'

'A tunnel,' added Milo.

Princess Ava looked at Jack, delight on her face.

'Really?' she said.

'Yes,' nodded Jack.

'Then what are we waiting for?' said Ava. 'Let's find this tunnel!'

# CHAPTER 3

Before they sprang into action, Ava insisted on returning to her caravan with Meenu to put on her Masked Avenger wrestling outfit.

'I can't go scrambling around in tunnels like this,' she pointed out, gesturing at her billowy frock. 'And say we come up against trouble? I need to be properly dressed for it.'

Ava and Meenu ran off through the busy campsite.

'Maybe I put my wrestling costume on as well,' suggested Big Rock.

'No,' said Jack. 'Your costume is already falling apart. Crawling through a tunnel could finish it off.'

'Crawling?' echoed Robin doubtfully.

'How small is this tunnel?'

'I've only seen the entrance, and that's pretty small,' said Jack.

'I could get stuck,' said Robin. 'And so could Big Rock.'

'I think it gets bigger once you're inside,' said Jack. 'The entrance was kept small to hide it.'

'You *think* it gets bigger?' queried Robin, still doubtful.

'We be okay,' said Big Rock confidently. 'Jack know what he doing.'

'I suppose so,' grumbled Robin. 'But what if this army of deadly creatures comes after us? It's all right for you. You're a troll made of rock. Deadly creatures just bounce off you. But I'm a horse, and we horses are made of . . . well . . .'

'Meat,' said Big Rock.

'Yes,' said Robin. 'Good-looking and clever – but made of meat. And therefore very much at risk from deadly creatures.'

Just then, Ava – now dressed in her Masked Avenger outfit – and Meenu reappeared.

'Right,' said the Masked Avenger. 'I'm ready! Lead on, Jack!'

'I was just saying –' Robin began to explain to her.

'Yes, all right, Robin,' said Jack. 'We'll make sure we're careful that no one notices us when we go to the tunnel. We don't want anyone following us, or sending a deadly army after us.'

'Really?' commented Robin sarcastically. 'Don't you think people might notice a huge troll, a girl in a masked wrestling costume, a horse, a phoenix and three others all sneaking off somewhere?'

'Actually, there's such a mixture of people here that we don't look out of place,' pointed out Meenu. 'Look. There are goblins, elves, orcs – and the humans here look weirder than any of them.'

'Good point,' said Jack. 'Okay, let's go.'

He led the gang away from the camp towards the small wood bordering the river that ran through the Veto Estate.

'The entrance to the tunnel is in the riverbank,' he explained to the Avenger and Meenu.

'Isn't that dangerous?' asked the Avenger. 'The river could flood into the tunnel.'

'Yes,' agreed Jack. 'But that's only ever happened a couple of times before.'

'You mean it *has* flooded?' said Robin, shocked.

'But not for years and years! It'll be fine!' insisted Jack.

As they neared the cluster of trees and bushes, they heard worried voices coming from just beyond it. They took cover behind the foliage and peered out.

Right ahead of them, in the riverbank, they could see a small, dark hole. The entrance to the secret tunnel! But standing next to it, their heads close together, talking, was a group of orcs. They were obviously upset. Jack guessed it was because they'd been abandoned by their master, Lord Veto, and were owed wages.

'Orcs,' muttered Milo. 'It looks like they know about the tunnel.'

'That doesn't surprise me,' said Jack. 'Orcs are sneaky.'

'But in that case, why are they hanging about? Why haven't they gone in?' asked Meenu.

'Because the tunnel is a very dangerous place,' said Jack. 'And most orcs are cowards.'

'Dangerous?' queried Robin nervously. 'You mean, because it's small and might flood?'

'That's not all . . .' admitted Jack.

'What are the other dangers?'

'Well, there are the ghosts,' said Jack.

Big Rock snorted. 'No such thing as ghosts!' he said.

'Yes, well, that's what people in the castle said about the tunnel. They said it was dangerous because of the ghosts and the giant rats.'

'*Giant* rats?' asked Robin.

'Yes,' nodded Jack. 'Huge ones. They said they're big enough and tough enough to eat orcs. And then there are the spiders.'

'Spiders?' shuddered Big Rock. 'Poisonous ones?'

'I don't know,' said Jack. 'I've never been in the tunnel. All I know is what I've heard about it, and that it comes out in the cellars of the castle.'

'Maybe we ought to leave it till tomorrow,' said Robin.

'Scared?' asked Meenu.

'Certainly not!' said Robin. 'It's just that rats can be very bad-tempered, and if there are a lot of them, and they eat orcs . . . Well . . .'

'Spiders,' said Big Rock unhappily. And Jack knew he was remembering the time he'd been bitten by poisonous spiders and nearly died.

'The problem is, how to get past the orcs and into the tunnel,' said Milo.

'No problem,' said Big Rock. 'Me and Masked Avenger deal with orcs.' And he made the fart noise he often made when talking about orcs, to show his displeasure about them.

'But there are ten orcs and just two of you,' pointed out Milo.

'Me and Masked Avenger beat ten orcs, no problem,' said Big Rock confidently.

'The problem is that a battle like that will cause a lot of noise, and that'll bring other people coming to find out what's going on . . .' said Meenu.

'And they'll find out about the tunnel,' finished Jack.

'I've got an idea,' said Robin. 'Why don't we –'

But before he could finish, there was the sound of rushing footsteps, and then an orc appeared, hurrying from the direction of the castle.

'There's a riot going on!' he shouted in panic at the orcs gathered by the tunnel entrance. 'People are talking about breaking into the castle to take stuff for what they're owed!'

'That was my idea!' complained Robin, upset. '*I* was going to suggest getting rid of the orcs by telling them that there was a riot going on and people were breaking into the castle!'

'It would have worked,' nodded Milo, as they saw the orcs rush off towards the castle, leaving just one lone orc on guard by the tunnel entrance.

'But it was *my* idea!' repeated Robin, really fed up.

'And now it's really happened,' said the Avenger. 'So, Big Rock: now there's one orc and two of us.'

'Good,' nodded Big Rock. 'I go talk to him.'

And Big Rock left their hiding place and strode to where the orc was standing guard.

'You! Orc!' said Big Rock. 'Go away!'

'No!' retorted the orc. 'I know who you are! You're Big Rock, the Wrestling Troll. Well, I'm

Dunk the Dangerous Orc and I'm telling you that you don't scare me, so –'

Before the orc could finish what he was saying, Big Rock had grabbed him with both of his huge hands, turned him upside down and crashed him head first onto the ground.

'Ow!' moaned the orc, dazed.

'Okay!' called out Big Rock to the others. 'I talk to him.'

'Yes, so we saw,' said Milo as the gang joined Big Rock by the fallen orc. They looked at the entrance to the tunnel – a smallish cave-like hole in the riverbank.

'Well, what are we waiting for?' said the Avenger. 'Let's go.'

And with that, she disappeared into the entrance.

'Okay,' said Jack. 'Everyone into the tunnel!'

# CHAPTER 4

One by one they squeezed their way in through the small entrance. Once they were inside, the tunnel became larger, just as Jack had said it would, and they were able to stand up in it. Tiny holes had been made in the ceiling to let in air from outside. They also let in some light so that, although the tunnel was dim and gloomy, they were still able to see.

'Well, so far nothing's attacked us,' said the Avenger.

'So far,' repeated Robin gloomily.

They moved forward cautiously, listening out for noises that might betray anything else that was in the tunnels with them – any of the dangers that Jack had mentioned.

'So far so good,' said Meenu.

They continued walking, but after they'd gone about a hundred metres, the tunnel seemed to get much darker.

'There's something right across the tunnel,' said Milo. 'It looks like a net curtain.'

They approached the hanging obstacle, and then stopped.

'It's a giant spider's web,' said Jack.

Big Rock stepped back.

'Hate spiders.' He shuddered.

'Actually, spiders are good creatures,' said Meenu. 'They eat flies and other insects that spread diseases. People shouldn't be frightened of them.'

'Unless they're very, *very* big,' said Jack nervously. He pointed. 'Like those.'

The others looked, and saw that about twelve huge spiders had crawled down from the ceiling onto the spider's web, and were making their way down to the floor of the tunnel. They were so big that the gang could see their eyes, and the hooked claws next to their gaping mouths.

'AAAAARGH!!!'

As one, they all shouted and stepped back in alarm. The next second there was a flash of bright light that lit up the tunnel as Blaze changed into a dragon. The dragon opened its mouth and let out a burst of flame, directed at the heavy spider's web. Immediately the spiders retreated, back to where they'd come from, scuttling away and disappearing into cracks in the rocks above them. A large hole, burnt by Blaze, had appeared in the heavy web.

'Thanks, Blaze,' said Jack, as the phoenix changed back to its normal shape.

'The spiders are still here,' said Milo apprehensively. 'They're hiding in the ceiling and the walls.'

'We've got Blaze with us if they come after us again,' said Jack.

'Don't like spiders,' grunted Big Rock.

They moved on. Jack noticed that Blaze kept cocking his head to one side, as if he were listening out for something.

'What's up, Blaze?' he asked.

'Something's following us,' whispered the phoenix.

'What?' asked Jack. 'The spiders?'

'Perhaps,' said Blaze. 'But I can't tell.'

Jack called for the others to stop, then motioned for them to gather round him. He whispered, 'Don't turn around, but we're being followed.'

'What by?' asked Big Rock, turning around to look.

'Jack said, "Don't turn around"!' snorted Robin.

'Ah,' said Big Rock. 'Anyway, I not scared. I go back and see who it is.'

And he turned to head back down the tunnel.

'It could be spiders,' said Jack.

Big Rock stopped.

'I wait and see,' he said.

'This is a really creepy place,' said Milo with a shudder.

'At least the only problems we've come up against have been those spiders,' said Meenu. 'If we're lucky, that'll be all we meet.'

'And if we're *un*lucky, we've still got the rats and the ghosts to come,' said Robin sourly.

'No such thing as ghosts,' said Big Rock.

# CHAPTER 5

They followed the tunnel as it twisted and turned. As they walked, Jack and Blaze kept their ears alert for whatever was following them; but either they'd stopped following them, or they were being very quiet about it.

The gang turned a bend and stopped as they came to a fork, where the tunnel branched in two directions.

'I think we ought to take the tunnel to the left,' said Milo.

'Why?' asked Robin.

'Because I just heard a noise coming from the tunnel to the right.'

They strained their ears and listened, and then they heard it too. A scuttling sound, along with a sharp, scratching noise.

'Spiders?' asked Meenu.

'That noise sounds a bit heavy for spiders,' said Jack. 'And what's making that scratching sound?'

'Claws,' said Blaze. 'Very sharp claws.'

'There's a swishing noise as well. Like something sweeping along the ground.'

'Long tails,' said the Avenger.

'Lots of long tails,' added Milo, listening.

'Blaze, I think we might need you in your dragon shape again, with lots of fire,' said Jack.

There was a flash of light as Blaze changed shape into the dragon once more. He opened his mouth and breathed out . . . but this time there was only a puff of black smoke – no flames.

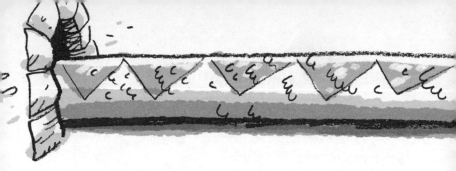

'I've used up too much energy changing to be able to make fire,' said Blaze.

'That's a pity,' said Milo nervously. 'Because the swishing and scratching and scuttling noises are getting nearer. And any second –'

'*SSSSS!*'

From out of the right-hand tunnel appeared a long, slithering snake. It had a wide mouth with sharp teeth, and a forked tongue that flicked in and out. Its eyes glowed yellow in the gloom. As he looked at it, Jack could feel himself getting sleepy.

'Don't look at its eyes!' shouted Meenu in

alarm. 'It's a hypnosnake!' And she turned her back on the creature, and then reached out and quickly pulled the Avenger's mask down over her eyes.

The snake's hypnotic gaze was having an effect on the others, too. Even Big Rock was looking dazed.

'You can't hypnotise me!' cried Robin, and the old horse poised himself to charge at the snake, but somehow his legs and his body began to feel so very heavy . . .

*WHOOOSHHH!!!*

Jack came out of his trance with a shock. He looked towards the tunnel on the right. The snake-like creature had gone.

'Who did it take?' he asked anxiously, looking around at the rest.

They were all still there: Milo, Big Rock, Robin, Blaze, the Masked Avenger and Meenu.

'What happened?' demanded the Avenger, straightening her mask so she could see again. 'Where did that thing go?'

'Something grabbed it and pulled it back into

the tunnel,' said Meenu. 'I saw it vanish out of the corner of my eye.'

'Whatever it was, we ought to be thankful to it for saving us,' said Milo.

'Or not,' said Robin.

'What do you mean?' asked the Avenger.

'Something that can do that to a creature like that sounds pretty big and dangerous to me.'

'Like what?' asked Big Rock.

'Well, we heard the sound of sharp claws, but that snake didn't have legs or claws. So whatever took that snake . . .'

'Is rat,' said Big Rock.

'We don't know that for sure,' said Meenu.

'Yes we do,' said Jack with a shudder and a gulp, and he pointed.

From out of the tunnel came a rat. Then another. Then another. And not just small rats, or even medium-sized rats. These were enormous rats, as big as dogs, with very sharp teeth glinting in the half-light, eyes shining, their coats glistening black and brown, and their very long tails swishing behind them.

# CHAPTER 6

'Okay,' said Milo. 'These are definitely the giant rats, and if you want my opinion, this is as far as we go.'

'No,' said Jack. 'I have to get inside the castle and get that ring.'

'Rats not hurt me,' said Big Rock. And he stepped towards the creatures, his fists bunched.

The rats let out a low growl and opened their mouths to bare their sharp teeth at the big troll as they advanced. Suddenly the leading rat leapt at Big Rock, claws and teeth bared.

*BOP!!*

The rat crumpled to the ground, out cold, as Big Rock's fist rammed into its snout. The other rats stopped their advance and looked down at the unconscious rat.

Good, hoped Jack. That will scare them away!

It didn't. Instead, more rats came rushing out of the tunnel, some leaping at Big Rock, the others aiming for the rest of the gang.

Jack grappled with a rat that jumped at him, his hands around its throat to keep its head away from him and stop its sharp teeth from biting him. Now would be a good time to turn into Thud, he told himself, but nothing was happening.

The Masked Avenger had grabbed one of the rats by its tail and was swinging it, banging it against the rocky side of the tunnel. Robin was kicking out hard with his hooves, sending rats falling back. Milo had jumped on the back of one rat while Meenu held onto its tail, the pair of them trying to bring it to the ground together.

Blaze had taken on the form of a huge grey rat and was battling, rat against rat, while Big Rock continued grabbing and punching. The rats obviously saw the troll as the main danger, because more of them joined in the attack on Big Rock.

Let me turn into Thud! begged Jack. But still nothing happened.

Suddenly Jack became aware that someone else – or some*thing* else – had become engaged in the battle and was pummelling the rats that hung onto Big Rock and hurling them aside.

And then there came a warning shout from Blaze. 'Look out!'

There was a huge rushing sound coming from the direction of the entrance behind them, and the next second the gang were engulfed in a wall of foaming, swirling water that lifted them off their feet and hurled them along, banging them against the sides and floor of the tunnel.

'It's the river!' shouted the Avenger. 'It's broken into the tunnel!'

Frantically, Jack fought to keep his head above water, but the force of the raging torrent pulled him down. He could feel the water filling his nose, choking him. No, he thought. I mustn't drown! I have to find that ring!

And then he felt a grab on his collar and found himself being hauled upwards, out of the water, and plonked down on a rocky ledge. Dazed, he opened his eyes and looked into the face of Dunk, the orc that Big Rock had hit outside the entrance to the tunnel.

Jack became aware that the others were also climbing onto the ledge, being helped up by Big Rock, who was standing, rock solid, in the racing water. The Masked Avenger and Meenu had hauled themselves out, while Robin swam to the ledge and was helped out by Milo, Big

Rock and a large grey rat, which turned back into Blaze once the old horse was safe.

'There are some steps here!' called the Avenger. 'They go up!'

And she ran to a doorway in the wall of the tunnel.

'Come on!' she called.

Meenu followed her, along with Milo, Robin and Blaze.

Jack turned back to the orc, who was still crouching on the ledge.

'You saved my life,' he said, surprised.

'Yes,' said Dunk.

'Why?' asked Jack.

'Because if I didn't, you'd have drowned,' said Dunk.

'But . . .' stammered Jack, still bewildered. He didn't understand this. All the orcs he'd known, especially those who worked for Lord Veto, had been nasty and vicious and were not to be trusted.

Big Rock hauled himself out of the water onto the ledge, then held out his hand towards Dunk.

'You help me fight rats,' he said. 'Save me. Thank you.'

Dunk took the troll's hand and shook it.

'I still don't understand why you helped us,' said Jack.

'Because I want to find Lord Veto,' said Dunk.

'Why?' asked Jack.

Dunk hesitated, then he announced: 'Because I want to tell him I quit. I've realised his sneaky ways have led me down the wrong path in life.

I've had enough! I thought you might be looking for him. If you find him, then I find him.'

'But if you want to quit, you could just leave now,' pointed out Meenu.

'Yes, but Lord Veto owes me back wages,' said Dunk. 'I intend to get them so I can start a new life.'

'So it was you who was following us?' asked Jack.

'Yes,' said Dunk.

'You good orc,' said Big Rock. 'Brave. I sorry I bang you to ground.'

'Yes, well, I'm sorry as well,' said Dunk. 'It hurt.'

'You can punch me,' offered Big Rock.

'No thank you,' said Dunk.

'Hurry up!' came the voice of the Avenger. 'I think we've found the way to the kitchens!'

# CHAPTER 7

Jack, Big Rock and Dunk scrambled up the steps and found the rest of the gang waiting impatiently for them. Robin looked at Dunk suspiciously.

'What's that orc doing with us?' he demanded.

'He saved my life,' said Jack. 'And he came to Big Rock's rescue when those rats were attacking us.'

'An *orc*?' said Robin.

'Yes,' said Jack.

Robin shook his head in astonishment. 'An orc doing good,' he said. 'I've never heard of such a thing.'

'I think the kitchens are this way,' said the Avenger, pointing.

'Yes, they are,' nodded Jack. 'I recognise this part of the castle. We're in the cellars. This must be the entrance to the tunnels.'

He set off at a run, the others following him, and soon they came to a door with the word KITCHENS on it.

Jack pushed open the door and stepped in, and then he stopped, as all the memories of his time working there as a kitchen boy flooded back. How long had it been since he was last here? A year. A long time. But coming back into the kitchen like this, seeing it all looking the same, it was as if it had only been yesterday.

The others crowded through the door behind Jack and stood looking around them, taking in the large kitchen with the two huge wooden tables in the centre of the room, and the old iron oven in the fireplace, blackened with age and heat. The oven was cold now – the wood fires inside it had been left to go out. Along one wall was a row of ancient sinks made of stone, with very old water taps above them.

'Is this where you worked?' asked Milo.

'This is where I lived,' Jack corrected him. 'I helped prepare food at those tables, and washed up the pots and pans and plates and cutlery in those sinks. And at night I slept in a basket in that corner.' And Jack pointed towards the far corner of the kitchen, where they could see a broken wicker basket. 'I can't believe it's still there. They didn't throw it out.'

He walked over to the corner of the room, the others following him. They stood looking

down at Jack's old bed: a ragged, round basket, lined with bits of old paper.

'I had a dog who had a better basket than that,' said the Avenger.

'Poor Jack,' sighed Meenu. 'It must have been horrible.'

'It was,' admitted Jack. Then he smiled. 'But I've got friends now. And that's what counts.'

He knelt down beside the basket, then reached out behind it and pushed his fingers into the gap between two of the bricks in the old, crumbling wall. The brick came out. Jack dropped the brick in the basket, and took out a tiny cloth parcel from the hiding place. He unfolded the cloth to reveal a silver ring. On it was a crest: a small picture of a shield, with what looked like two stones either side.

'This is it,' said Jack.

'Ha!' exclaimed Big Rock, excitedly. 'Me look, Jack?'

'Here,' said Jack, and he handed the ring to Big Rock.

The giant troll examined the ring, and then gave it back to Jack.

'That Royal Troll Ring,' he said.

'What do you mean, Royal Troll Ring?' asked Meenu.

'Shield on it,' said Big Rock. 'Shield of Troll King.'

'I didn't know there was a Troll King,' said Milo.

'There not, no more,' said Big Rock. 'When Troll King died, he last one. No more Troll Royal Family.'

'But why did my mother leave this to me?' asked Jack, studying the ring.

'Maybe she Troll Princess,' said Big Rock. 'You half-troll, Jack.'

'But what would a Troll Princess be doing at Veto Castle?' asked Milo.

'Perhaps you'd better ask Lord Veto,' hissed a voice.

# CHAPTER 8

They spun round and saw a shadowy figure, standing in the doorway. It was very tall and thin, and covered from head to foot in some sort of black material.

'It's a ghost!' exclaimed Robin.

'No such thing as ghost!' snorted Big Rock, and he strode towards the figure.

Immediately the figure produced a long sword with a wickedly sharp-looking blade.

'Sword not hurt me!' snapped Big Rock.

But before the troll could do anything, the shadowy figure had moved – it was now standing with the sword pointing at the Masked Avenger's throat.

'No,' said the figure. 'But it'll hurt her.'

'I didn't see it move!' whispered Dunk, shocked.

'Because it's a ghost!' repeated Robin, awed.

'No,' said the Avenger. 'It's a ninja. One of the deadly assassins I told you about. They can use anything and everything as weapons. They move as silently as ghosts.'

'He only one,' snorted Big Rock.

'Er . . . two,' said Robin.

'Three,' said Blaze.

They looked towards the door, where more figures, dressed in the same way and holding long swords that glinted in the half-light, had appeared.

'I count six,' muttered Milo.

'Me too,' agreed Jack.

'If you do as we say, you live,' said the first ninja. 'If you resist, you die.'

'We live,' said Robin.

'Me and Masked Avenger beat them!' said Big Rock firmly.

'While the rest of us are chopped into little pieces,' said Milo unhappily. 'No, we have to give in, Big Rock. For the moment.'

'What did you mean when you said, "Ask Lord Veto"?' Jack addressed the first ninja, puzzled.

'Follow and you'll find out,' said the ninja. 'But any tricks from the troll, or anyone else, and you'll all die.'

'No tricks, Big Rock,' Milo said.

'Okay,' nodded the troll.

Three of the ninjas left the kitchen and stood in the corridor outside, swords ready, while the gang came out, followed by the final three ninjas. As they walked along the corridor, aware of the armed ninjas beside them, Milo whispered in a low voice, 'Any chance of turning into Thud and getting us out of this, Jack?'

'It wouldn't do much good if he did,' whispered the Avenger. 'Ninjas are the fastest creatures ever known. By the time Jack turned into Thud, most of us would already be dead. These guys are *fast*!'

'These guys also have excellent hearing,' snapped the ninja nearest them. 'Even when you whisper.'

They walked on down the corridor.

'We're going to the dungeons,' said Jack.

'Yes,' said the ninja.

The ninja stopped at a door and opened it. 'Everyone in,' it said. 'Except you.' And it pointed the sharp tip of its sword blade at Jack.

'No!' shouted Big Rock. 'You not kill Jack!'

'Yes. If you kill him, you'll have to kill me as well!' shouted Milo.

Robin sighed.

'Oh well,' he said unhappily. 'I suppose if we're doing that "One for all, all for one" stuff . . .'

'No,' said Jack. 'If they were going to kill me, they'd have done it already.'

'You're right,' hissed the ninja. 'If you behave, you will all stay alive, until our Master tells us what to do with you.'

'Your Master?' queried the Avenger. 'Who's your Master?'

'In,' said the ninja, and gestured with the sword at the door to the empty cell.

All the gang except Jack filed in.

'It's going to be a bit crowded in here,' complained Dunk.

'Tough,' said the ninja, and it slammed the door shut then drew the two heavy bolts across on the outside.

'Stay here and guard,' the ninja ordered three of its comrades.

As they took up their positions outside the cell door, the head ninja snapped at Jack: 'This way.'

Flanked by the three remaining ninjas, Jack walked along the corridor to another door, about fifty metres further on. The head ninja unbolted the door and swung it open.

'In,' it said.

Jack stepped in, and was shocked to see two figures sitting on a bench, who jumped to their feet as he came in. They were Lord Veto and Warg.

The cell door clanged shut, and Jack heard the bolts slide back into place. He glared at Veto and Warg.

'So!' he said. '*You're* their Master!'

'Of course I'm not, you idiot!' raged Lord Veto. 'If I was, do you think I'd be locked in this cell?'

'Yes I do,' said Jack. 'It's so you can be safe from the Voyadis.'

'Those ninjas *are* the Voyadis!' stormed Lord Veto. 'Or, at least, they work for them! They've locked me up in here, and they're going to take terrible revenge on me! They're going to slice me up and feed me to goblins!'

'They said they'd slice us *both* up, my Lord,' said Warg.

'*You?*' sneered Lord Veto. 'You don't count. You're just an orc! I am Lord Veto!'

'Soon to be Lord Goblinmeat,' said Jack sarcastically.

'But you can change that, Jack,' said Lord Veto, his face forcing a smile. 'I know you can turn into that fierce giant troll, Thud. You can turn into him and break us out of here. You can save me, Jack!'

'Why would I want to save you?' demanded Jack. 'You kept me working here in the castle as a slave, right from when I was a tiny boy. You didn't feed me properly, you didn't clothe me. I was cold and hungry. I slept in a basket in the kitchen!'

'A nice warm place to sleep,' purred Lord Veto.

'No, it wasn't!' shouted Jack. 'At night the fire went out and it was cold! And then, finally, you just threw me out in the rain without a penny!'

'I was upset at the time, Jack,' appealed Lord Veto. 'I wasn't myself.'

'Yes, you were yourself!' retorted Jack. 'Cruel. Selfish. Nasty. Unfeeling. That's what you are!' And Jack moved closer to Lord Veto and glared at him. 'So, bearing all that in mind, can you think of one reason why I should lift one finger to save you?'

Lord Veto hesitated, his eyes avoiding Jack's as he scowled unhappily. Finally he looked Jack in the face and announced firmly: 'Because I am your grandfather.'

# CHAPTER 9

Jack stared at Lord Veto.

It couldn't be true! This was another lie, a sneaky trick by Lord Veto.

'No!' he shouted. 'That's not possible!'

'Yes it is, Jack,' said Lord Veto. 'Warg knows the truth, too.'

Jack looked at the orc, who nodded.

'Warg will say anything you want him to say,' said Jack.

Lord Veto fell silent for a second, then he asked, 'Did you find it, Jack?'

'Find what?'

'The thing you came back for. Hidden behind that brick by your basket in the kitchen. The ring.'

Jack stared at Veto, shocked. Lord Veto nodded solemnly.

'I've always known it was there. But I let you keep it.' He gave a sigh. 'I suppose I'm just an old sentimentalist.'

'You! Sentimental!' scoffed Jack. 'You haven't any feelings!'

'I did once, Jack,' said Lord Veto sadly. 'I had a daughter called Leonora. She was your mother, and I loved her very much.'

Jack was unable to take his eyes off Lord Veto. Could he be telling the truth? Or was it another of Lord Veto's ploys?

'Unfortunately, she fell in love with a troll.'

And then Jack recalled the shield design on the silver ring in his pocket, and what Big Rock had said about it. 'The troll she fell in love with was a Prince!' he said.

'Yes, but a *Troll* Prince! What use is a Troll Prince? Trolls don't care about the important things in life, like money, or social position . . .'

'What happened to them?'

'I forbad Leonora to have anything to do

with this troll,' said Veto. 'I went to see the Troll Prince's father, the Troll King, and told him it was an unsuitable match. A troll and a human! Unthinkable! He agreed with me. He had other plans for a wife for his son.'

'But they had me.'

'Yes,' growled Lord Veto. 'Leonora defied me, and the Troll Prince defied his father, and they ran away together. The Troll King disowned his son. But I put out a search for them, determined to bring my daughter back home. It took me a year of searching, but finally my

orcs learnt where the couple were living, and that they had a child.'

'Me,' said Jack.

'Yes,' said Lord Veto. 'I set out with my orcs to bring my daughter back. She didn't want to come. When my orcs tried to take her, the Troll Prince . . .' Veto hesitated, '. . . he resisted.'

'You killed him,' said Jack accusingly. 'You killed my father!'

'It was an accident!' cried Lord Veto. 'We caught up with them at the top of a very high cliff. There was a struggle and he . . . fell. Even trolls die when they fall from that height.

'I brought Leonora and you back here to Veto Castle. I thought she'd be able to start a new life. Forget about the Troll Prince.' Suddenly Lord Veto looked very sad, and very old. 'The stupid girl! She told me she was going to run away, so I had to keep her locked up in her room in the castle. I thought if I took you away from her and she didn't see you, it would help her forget about the Troll Prince. So I gave you to one of the kitchen women to look after.' He shook his head. 'Leonora became more and more unhappy. She refused to eat. And . . .' Lord Veto's eyes closed, and Jack thought he could see a tear glinting on his cheek. Veto finished with, '. . . she died.'

'She died of a broken heart!' said Jack. 'You killed her!'

'I could have given her everything!' retorted Lord Veto angrily.

'Except the things she really wanted: the ones she loved.'

'Love!' scoffed Lord Veto. 'What good is love? Does it earn money?'

'Why did you keep me?' asked Jack.

'Because you were my grandson!'

'But you were cruel to me! You kept me working in your kitchen and sleeping in a basket. You treated your animals better than you treated me.'

'Because I hated you!' grated Veto. 'Every time I looked at you, I thought of my daughter and what had happened to her, and I blamed you! It was all your fault!'

As Jack glared at Lord Veto he could feel anger rising up inside him like he'd never felt before. Because of this man, his father and mother had died. Then Lord Veto had kept him as a slave for the whole of his young life, and just discarded him into a rainy night without a thought for him. Tears of pain and rage sprang to his eyes, blinding him. No, not tears, something harder, something shale-like; and he was growing, filling the cell, looking down on the upturned and terrified faces of Lord Veto and Warg . . .

'*GRAAAAARRRRR!!!!!!!!*'

He kicked out, overwhelmed by anger, but he managed to turn away from Lord Veto just in time and his foot smashed into the cell door, sending it crashing out into the corridor.

Thud leapt out of the cell, and as he did so the ninjas on guard sprang at him, brandishing their swords.

*CRASH!!! SNAP!*

The giant Thud snatched the swords from all three and broke them as if they were matchsticks.

Then his huge arm swung in an arc, swatting all three ninjas and sending them sprawling to the ground, unconscious.

The other three ninjas ran towards Thud, swords raised, from their position outside the other cell door. But before they could advance, Thud had rushed to them, his huge fists swinging. The three ninjas slashed at Thud, but their swords shattered on the troll's rocky body.

*BANG! BANG! BANG!*

The three ninjas crumpled to the ground alongside their fallen comrades as Thud's fists connected.

'*GRAAAAR!!*'

Thud let out another yell of rage and kicked at the door of the other cell. The door buckled, and the huge troll flew into the cell, skidded across the floor and smacked into the opposite wall.

Robin looked at the open doorway, and then at the shrinking figure of Thud, now being replaced by the tiny, frail person of Jack.

'You could have just pulled the bolts open,' he complained. 'That flying door nearly hit me.'

'Sorry,' said Jack. 'But I've just had some bad news.' He looked at them and then said helplessly, 'Lord Veto's my grandfather.'

# CHAPTER 10

They listened in stunned silence as Jack told them what Lord Veto had said. After he had finished, they carried on looking at Jack in the same stunned silence. It was Blaze who broke the awkward hush.

'That's so sad,' he said.

'Are you sure he wasn't lying to you?' asked Robin. 'Lord Veto lies all the time.'

'No,' said Jack. 'I knew as he was saying it that it was the truth.' He hesitated, then said quietly, 'I could see it in his face. In his eyes. It's the truth.'

'You Troll King,' said Big Rock. And he bent low and bowed to Jack.

'What?' asked Dunk.

'Jack son of Troll Prince. Prince only son of Troll King. Jack heir to Troll Throne.'

'No!' said Jack quickly. 'I'm not a proper troll. I'm only a half-troll!'

'You King,' said Big Rock.

'Wow!' said the Masked Avenger, staring at Jack with awe. 'Big Rock's right.'

'No!' repeated Jack, but even more seriously. And he looked at the others and said very firmly: 'This has got to be a secret between all of us. No one else must know about it.'

Robin looked at Dunk suspiciously.

'I know *I* won't say anything, if that's what you want . . .' Robin began.

'That's what I want,' nodded Jack.

'. . . and I'm sure none of the others will. But what about *him*? He's an orc! And we know they're not to be trusted.'

'I trust him,' said Jack.

'And me,' said Big Rock. 'He save me.'

'Not all orcs are sneaky and cheat,' said Dunk. 'That's how Lord Veto ordered us to be when we wrestled for him. Like I told you,

I'd begun to think that wasn't the right way to live. And now I've seen how you guys are together . . . Well, it's definitely a nicer way to be. And I promise I won't say anything about your secret. Not until you tell me I can.' And he looked appealingly at Jack, and added, 'Because I'd love to tell someone this! It's so fantastic!'

'No,' said Jack again.

'Okay,' nodded Dunk. He sighed. 'I'll keep my snout shut.' Then he asked thoughtfully, 'By the way, has anyone checked if Lord Veto is still here?'

That shook everyone out of their stunned amazement at learning Jack's story, and they all rushed out of the cell and along the corridor.

The cell where Lord Veto and Warg had been was empty. The corridor was also empty. The ninjas had gone.

'What happened to the ninjas?' asked Milo.

'They failed, so there's only one course of action they can take,' said the Avenger.

'What?' asked Big Rock.

'They run away and hide.' The Avenger shrugged. 'They've failed, so now the Voyadis will be after them.'

'And they'll be after Lord Veto,' said Milo.

'And they'll be after Jack,' added Meenu unhappily.

'Why?' asked Robin.

'Because they'll work out that someone helped Lord Veto escape. And when they ask around, they'll find out that we were all here when it happened. And when they discover that the ring has gone from behind that brick in the kitchen . . .'

'But how will the Voyadis know that's anything to do with Jack? How would they even know the ring existed?' asked Milo.

'Because the Voyadis know *everything*,' said the Avenger. 'That's their real power! I bet they even know about Jack being the half-troll grandson of Lord Veto.'

'What makes you think that?' asked Jack.

'Remember what that ninja said to you when he first appeared? "Ask Lord Veto." Lord Veto must have tried to make a deal with them before they locked him up. He would have told them everything.'

'So your secret's out anyway, Jack,' said Dunk cheerfully. 'So now I can tell people!'

'No,' said the Avenger. 'The Voyadis will be keeping it to themselves. That's the way they work. So we'll all respect what Jack wants and keep it a secret, too.'

'I wonder if the water's gone from the tunnel yet,' said Robin.

'I'll check,' said Blaze. And he turned into a rat and scurried off.

'And then we can all get out of here,' said Jack, pleased at the prospect of leaving it all behind him.

'Yes, Majesty,' said Big Rock, and he gave a low bow to Jack again.

'Please stop that, Big Rock,' said Jack. 'I'm just Jack. I'm not the Troll King.'

'No, Majesty,' said Big Rock.

And he bowed low again.

# CHAPTER 11

Jack and Milo waved goodbye to Princess Ava and Meenu as their caravan trundled out through the gates of Veto Castle. The pair were heading back to Weevil.

No one else in the grounds seemed to take any notice of the caravan's departure. All the others – goblins, elves, orcs and humans – were too busy trying to get as near to the castle as possible, in readiness for when the doors opened for the auction.

'We ought to be getting on our way as well,' said Milo, 'now our business here is done.'

Jack looked towards their caravan, where Big Rock was putting a soft cushion on the driving seat for him.

'I wish he wouldn't do that,' sighed Jack. 'I can't convince him I'm not the Troll King.'

'Technically, you are,' said Milo.

'No, I'm not. I'm Jack,' said Jack.

'Yes, you are,' said Robin, joining them. 'I recognise you. You are the true Troll King . . .'

'Oh, don't *you* start!' said Jack grumpily.

'It was a joke,' said Robin defensively.

'And not a very funny one,' said Jack.

Big Rock joined them.

'Cushion in place, your Royal Highness,' he said.

'Big Rock, I am not –' began Jack. Then he saw the happy look on the troll's face and stopped. 'Thank you, Big Rock,' he said.

Blaze and Dunk joined them.

'I said to Dunk he could come with us if he wanted,' said Blaze.

The others looked at the phoenix in surprise, and then at Dunk. Then Robin nodded and said, 'Yes, he can. Why not? A Wrestling Troll and a Wrestling Orc on the same team. We can try that out at the next tournament we go to! That would be something to see!'

Dunk shook his head.

'Thanks for the offer,' he said. 'But I've decided to stop being a wrestler, or a bodyguard. I'm going back to my parents to work on the family farm.'

Robin stared at Dunk, his mouth dropping open.

'Farming orcs?' he said, stunned.

'Not all orcs are warriors,' said Dunk. 'We're very good at growing things too.' He gestured towards a group of orcs watching them. 'I'll wait here with the other orcs until the auction's over and see if we get the back pay we're owed, then I'll set off for home.'

With that, Dunk headed towards the other orcs, and soon they all had their heads together and were talking animatedly.

'Right, then, I suppose we can go,' said Milo. 'Everyone ready?'

'Hitch me up,' said Robin.

As Milo hitched the old horse to the caravan, Big Rock lifted Jack up and placed him gently on the cushion on the driving seat.

'There, your Majesty,' he said.

'Thank you, Big Rock,' said Jack.

'Right,' said Milo. 'Let's go!'

Robin gave a heave and the caravan, with Milo and Jack on board, rolled forward, while Big Rock trotted along beside it and Blaze flew overhead.

As it rolled out through the gates of Veto Castle, a figure dressed completely in black appeared from behind a tree, then was joined by another.

'We have to save our reputation,' said one of the ninjas.

'And save our lives,' said the other. 'If we capture Lord Veto and bring him to the Voyadis, they might forgive us.'

'So why are we following a caravan full of Wrestling Trolls?'

'Because they are connected to Lord Veto. Sooner or later they will find him, or he will find them. And when they meet, we will take him.'

'And what will we do about the Wrestling Trolls? Especially the big one who knocked us out and broke our swords?'

'We kill him,' said the ninja. 'We kill them all.'

HOT
KEY
BOOKS

Thank you for choosing a Hot Key book.

If you want to know more about our authors
and what we publish, you can find us online.

You can start at our website

**www.hotkeybooks.com**

And you can also find us on:

**We hope to see you soon!**

Lovereading4kids reader reviews of
**Wrestling Trolls Match 1: Big Rock and the Masked Avenger**
by Jim Eldridge

'I really like Wrestling Trolls. I really like Robin the horse because he talks, Big Rock because he's nice, Jack because he saves Princess Ava, and Princess Ava because she wrestles!'

Richie, age 7

'Wrestling Trolls is an action-packed book with awesome wrestling moves. The characters are clever and funny. I loved the story and can't wait to read the next instalment.'

Jacob, age 9

'The story had funny parts, action and good characters. Some of my favourite parts were Jack turning into a wrestling troll and I liked Robin the horse because he was grumpy and helpful.'

Jack, age 8

'It was brilliant! I liked how Jack changed into Thud - I won't tell you what Thud is so I don't give away the story . . . I really liked the song and keep singing it.'

George, age 7

'Wrestling Trolls is exciting because it is full of action. This book is fantastic if you like lots of wrestling and people being rescued from bad guys.'

Thomas, age 7

'I give it 10/10 even though I don't like wrestling, because I liked the story!'

Alexander, age 8